A Way With Words

Patsy Collins

The author can be found at
www.patsycollins.co.uk

ISBN: 978-1-914339-29-5

Contents

1. Easy Way Out

Anya screwed up the pretty invitation cards and hurled them towards the bin. "What a waste of money!" she said.

"I'd have done them if you'd just waited a minute," Stavros, her husband replied.

"No. I can't keep taking the easy way out by letting you make all the arrangements and do all the paperwork." As usual their conversation was conducted in Greek.

Anya collected up the ruined cards, and the sheet from which she'd tried to copy the neighbours' names, and put them in the recycling bin, just as she'd learned she was supposed to. She sighed; since arriving in England from Greece that was about all she had learned. Anya had concentrated on decorating their flat and caring for the children. She must overcome her poor spoken, and non-existent written, English.

Still, perhaps calling on the neighbours and inviting them to dinner would be friendlier; less formal. It was friends she wanted so a friendly approach made sense.

Once the children were in bed, Anya left Stavros watching TV and knocked gently on the door of the flat to her right. She wasn't at all sure the young occupants would accept her invitation as they seemed to have a busy social life, but they seemed pleasant and might appreciate being asked.

The door was soon opened. "Hello, Anya isn't it?" Sue asked.

"Hello. Yes. I cook dinner Friday. You and husband come please?"

"Oh, how kind! I'll just check with Dave what we're doing. Come in for a minute."

Anya followed her into a very tidy, but colourless home.

Once Anya repeated her invitation Dave said, "That sounds like fun. We usually go for a curry on a Friday. It'll be nice to have a change. What time do you want us?"

"Seven please. Early so children sleep after."

"That's fine," Sue said. "We'll bring a bottle."

Encouraged by their response, Anya visited the flat to her left. She was more nervous about visiting Elizabeth Walters as she felt she had more to lose. Elizabeth was a full time mum and housewife too; Anya hoped they'd become friends.

"Hello, Elizabeth."

Her neighbour's smile suggested Anya hadn't made too much of a mess in pronouncing the unfamiliar name.

"I cook dinner Friday. You and husband come please."

"Oh we'd love to, but I'm not sure if we'll be able to get a baby sitter in time."

"You have baby?"

Elizabeth laughed. "No! Two children are enough. A baby sitter is what we call someone who comes and looks after your children if you go out."

"No need baby sit. My boys here also. Your children eat also. I cook lots."

"Thank you. We'll be looking forward to it. What time shall we come round?"

"Seven please."

"That's fine. Would you like me to bring anything?"

"Well yes. For sitting, er … not baby, just sitting. Not enough …" she trailed of unable to remember the words Stavros had tried to teach her.

"Oh! You've not got enough seats for everyone?"

"I not know words."

"You need more things to sit on? Chairs?

Anya nodded.

"No problem, we'll bring our own."

Anya spent two days tracking down the ingredients she required. Aubergines, hummus, Retsina and vine leaves were not prominently on display in the local supermarket.

"Please, the thing from a vine," she asked and was shown first the drinks section and then offered sultanas.

Once she'd bought the familiar ingredients, creating her favourite recipes was simple. She sang a traditional Greek folk song to herself as she salted aubergines, chopped herbs and crushed garlic.

"Wow that smells amazing," Dave said as Stavros let him and his wife in.

"Your flat looks fabulous too," Sue added. "I love all the vibrant colours. You'd never know it was identical to ours under all the paint and tapestries and what are these, gourds?"

Before Stavros could reply, Elizabeth and her family arrived, carrying spare chairs. They too remarked on the lovely aroma and attractive decor.

There was chatter and laughter as Anya's guests squeezed around her dining table and helped themselves to wine or juice. With just a touch of ceremony, Anya carried the food to the table.

"Looks great, Anya," Dave said. "Sue and I have never eaten traditional Greek food before. We're really looking forward to the experience."

Soon conversation was reduced to words of praise for Anya's cooking.

"Thank you." Anya felt herself blush.

"How long have you lived over here?" Elizabeth asked.

"Two months," Stavros said.

"Your English is excellent," Dave said.

Stavros explained, "I had an English grandfather who taught me the language. I started teaching my boys before we moved and after only two months they've caught up with their classmates."

Anya nodded in agreement; she was proud of her family.

"My beautiful wife has many talents. Her cooking, as you know. Sewing," Stavros pointed to a beautifully embroidered wall hanging. "And poetry. In Greece she won competitions and her poems were printed every week in the local newspaper."

Anya was happy they joined in the praise, but even more pleased she seemed to have made friends.

The following day, Anya with recipe book in hand, visited Elizabeth.

"Hi, come in," said Elizabeth. "Do you have time for a cup of tea?"

"Yes, thank you."

They walked through to the kitchen where Elizabeth filled the kettle.

"I remembers you enjoy my mousaka. And ask about the vegetables and herbs. I have recipe, is Greek written. I read and you write? You have pen?"

"I haven't got time for that. Actually I think you'd better go."

Anya couldn't understand why the other woman was upset. Later she saw Elizabeth go out. Maybe she'd remembered something and it wasn't Anya's fault she was unhappy?

A man rang her bell and handed her a parcel and a book for her to sign.

"Sign and date in line three please, love."

She stared at the book.

"Put your name just there." He indicated an empty space.

She scribbled her name and he left.

Anya soon realised the contents weren't hers. Instead of embroidery silks, as expected, the box contained what she guessed were music CDs. Anya studied the label, realising the name was wrong. She found a bill and compared the addresses. They were the same, except for one letter in the row after the name. She'd show Stavros later, he'd read the delivery note and know who it belonged to.

Two hours later the door bell sounded again. It was Elizabeth.

"Could I have my package?" She said, holding up an orange card.

Anya fetched it and explained she'd opened the box by mistake.

"Even though my name and address are clearly written on it?" She tapped the large, neatly printed, label. "Can't the great poet read then?"

"Not English."

"Not so clever now are we? I might not get stuff in the papers or have kids that can learn a new language in a couple of months, but I can read my own name when it's looking me in the face."

Elizabeth grabbed her parcel, ignoring Anya's confused apology.

Anya sighed. She'd angered her neighbour again and looked stupid, because she'd been worried about writing in the delivery man's book.

"Stavros, I no take easy ways out," Anya announced when her husband returned from work. "I learn the English."

"Your English is fine, Anya. You're getting so used to it you even speak it to me sometimes."

"For practice. Us speak it all times, so I learn. I can't read or write. People not liking me because thinking I is stupid. I learn the reading and writing."

Stavros obtained details of adult literacy classes. Anya memorised the name and address of the teacher. She had to; Stavros was working away until after the first lesson.

"I'll send a postcard, written in English for you to practise with."

"Be careful how you say, I not want embarrass

teacher."

After Stavros left, Anya realised she didn't know what time the classes started. The boys were at school and Dave and Sue would be at work. Perhaps if she explained and asked for her help, Elizabeth would be kind.

She knocked on the door and showed Elizabeth the leaflet giving the course details. "Please, I do learning English. I not know when. You tell please?"

"I haven't got my glasses on, leave that here and I'll let you know."

That evening Elizabeth returned the leaflet. "Classes start at half past two tomorrow afternoon. You'll need to catch the number 47 bus at quarter to."

"Thank you, Elizabeth. Nice it is for you telling me."

"Not really. You're the nice one and I'd like us to be friends."

"You come now? Do drinking tea and being friend of me?"

"Yes, OK. Thanks."

Anya made tea and the two women sat on Anya's brightly coloured couch to drink it.

"I'm sorry I was rude, Anya. I'm jealous."

"I not understand."

"There's the fancy food you make. I have to stick to plain stuff. I'm jealous of your bright kids too, they write stories and cards for you. My kids don't show me anything they write. I don't have many friends either, I've moved since school and I'm no good at keeping in touch."

"Elizabeth, I not know this. It is sad, what you say."

"No. Ridiculous, that's what it is."

"Ridiculous? I not know this word."

Elizabeth quickly drank most of her tea, then put down her mug. "I've made my own problems, then when you tried to be friendly I pushed you away, in case you discovered my secret."

"Secret?"

Elizabeth picked up her mug, swirling the dregs of tea around.

"Elizabeth, I like try be your friend. Help each other?"

"Good idea, we could go to this class together," Elizabeth said, indicating the leaflet. "I can't read or write, that's why I can't follow a recipe, help my kids with homework, or contact friends. It's not easy you know, keeping illiteracy hidden. I'm going to take the easy way out, and learn."

2. One Day

The tutor's unusual first name might seem insufficient reason for me to book myself onto a day long writing workshop, but it's why I'm here. Elodie Marlett certainly sounds like a writer and she's made an effort to look like one too. Her strawberry blonde hair is piled up on her head, she's draped in scarves and wearing a floaty skirt.

She's quite a contrast to the rest of us. We're nearly all much older and have dressed more practically for the cold, wet day. The tea and coffee, available on arrival as promised, are very welcome to warm our chilled fingers before we begin putting them to use. The biscuits are popular too. No chocolate wafers, but plenty of other choices.

Once everyone has a drink and a seat, Elodie introduces herself. I listen intently, but not for the details of her publishing success; I'm not much of a reader. Then it's our turn to say a few words about ourselves. Thankfully there's nobody here I know, I'm nervous enough without that. Some of the others seem to have done a bit of writing before. Most hope to get published. I have hopes of my own, but they don't involve fame and fortune.

"I'm Margaret and I just thought I'd try something different," I mumble when it's my turn. That's true in a way.

Elodie is quietly confident as she points out the fire exits and explains what will happen during the day.

Maybe the wedding ring on her finger helps explain that? She probably feels loved and secure. Lucky her. Does that make me sound jealous? Perhaps I am a little, but that's not because I begrudge her happiness.

"I'm not one for too many rules," she tells us. "I'll be setting a variety of exercises, but you may get carried away with an idea or particular piece of writing. If that happens just go with it."

That won't happen with me. I'm not here for the writing.

"The important thing is to write, even if what you're doing differs from what everyone else is working on. Actually, especially if that's the case. Remember, I'm here to help, not judge."

Will she judge me I wonder?

We start off with some stuff about generating ideas and constructing plots. I'm surprised to find it's quite fun to make things up, especially as I don't intend to ever work on my crazy ideas. Even if this does turn out to have been a complete waste of time, I shan't be too sorry I came.

I'd agonised over whether to try to talk to Elodie in the lunch break, if she was really who I thought she was. All that fretting for nothing; I'm still no closer to being sure and in any case so many people are clustered around asking questions, either about her writing or their own, that it will be impossible for me to have a quiet word.

"This afternoon we're going to be bringing our characters to life," Elodie tells us. "You want the reader to see them, but we're not talking photographs here. I'll use my husband as an example. He's five foot nine, has light brown, very straight hair and hazel eyes. That doesn't tell you much, does it?"

Most of the class agree with her. I do see what she means. Lots of people fit that description, but even so, I can picture my son so clearly it's difficult for me to just sit here and listen politely. Elodie is Geraint's wife, I'm sure of it. A neighbour told me he married someone by that name, but until today I hadn't been sure it was true. I suppose the surname she uses is her pen name.

"How would you improve upon that description?" she asks us.

There are a few tentative suggestions about adding details, comparisons, action, similes and showing not telling. I don't follow it all. Elodie says to ask if anything isn't clear, but what I want to know has nothing to do with metaphors and adjectives.

"OK then. How about a lady who needs a step to reach the things in the back of her kitchen cupboard and whose clothes seem to all shrink while hanging in the wardrobe. Her hair is the colour of a winter sky. Can you see her?"

"Whenever I look in the mirror!" someone says.

Several others say it could be them. It could almost be me, but I don't say so.

"There's not really any more detail there than in my first description, but it was enough that a few of you felt you could either visualise or relate to her." Elodie explains why that's important to people writing stories and how it can be done, then sets us to 'building up and fleshing out' a character. "You can use one of those I've described, or create one of your own. Make me feel I know them."

I pick Geraint; of course I do. She knows him, better than I do now, but I'm not sure I have the literary skills to show her that. I think back, wanting to recall something typical and non controversial. There's the way, when offered a cup of tea, he always said, 'Oh, all right then' as though doing me a huge favour. In a way he was. He knew I liked to look after him, make a bit of a fuss of my only child. Since he was quite small it's been just the two of us you see. Along with the tea, I often gave him one of his favourite chocolate wafers. He was young and energetic enough to be able to eat whatever he liked, confident he'd burn it all off.

It's only as Elodie asks us to stop writing that I realise I've started.

One by one the attendees read their pieces and Elodie makes notes. She says something nice about each, then adds a little suggestion to improve or expand it. We're invited to do the same. Some take up the offer, mostly saying something like 'that was really good' with one or two repeating a few words from Elodie's earlier advice.

I'm nervous as I read, but not because I fear anyone being unkind. For one thing, I'm not expecting anyone to be impressed, and for another they all seem to be reacting to each other's efforts in the way they hope their own words will be greeted. Even if they think my writing poor, I know they'll listen politely until the end and try to think of something positive to say.

When I get to Geraint's 'Oh, go all right then' Elodie stops making notes and looks right at me. We have the same eyes, Geraint and I. She's staring into mine, but I think perhaps she sees his. I read the rest without glancing up again. There's a short silence when I finish, until Elodie speaks.

"That was very vivid, Margaret. I felt I could see and hear him."

Her words are those of teacher trying to encourage student, but her expression shows me she's learned something too – the truth about my relationship to her husband.

A few of the students say my description is 'interesting' or that my character sounds nice, but it's clear they wouldn't know Geraint if he walked in now and helped himself to a drink.

We attempt more exercises and then Elodie reads something about Geraint that's she's worked on while we were writing. It fits the lesson, so I don't know for sure that she wrote it just for me. To tell me how Geraint is now, that he still eats chocolate wafers and sometimes looks wistful as he undoes the wrapper. As though there's something missing that chocolate can't replace. But if she didn't want me to know, she'd have picked a different subject, wouldn't she? I begin to hope.

"I suppose you were expecting the break for coffee and cake about now?" Elodie asks.

Everyone assures her that's correct.

"You can have your refreshments, but I don't want you to stop working," Elodie says. "I'd like you to work on some of your exercises, placing one of the characters you've written about this afternoon into a plot line you created this morning. Try to create a complete scene, perhaps even a very short story. Is everyone happy with that? Anyone need help?"

A few tentative hands go up. One woman had done a creepy bit about someone going under a spooky, perhaps haunted, bridge. Elodie suggests explaining why the character is taking that route and not going round. "If she has to because she can't be late, or because something compels her, you'll add even more tension. It will be scarier because we'll see she won't choose another path at the last minute."

I see that's helped; the writer looks eager to start. Elodie makes suggestions to the others who ask for it. Then, as some start writing and others collect their cake and refill their cups, she approaches me.

"Will you be writing about your son?" she asks.

"Yes." How can I not? I can't think about anything other than the possibility of reaching out to him.

"You wrote in the past tense. Perhaps you'd like to say what's changed and why, and maybe how you feel about that?" Elodie suggests.

I can only nod.

Once we're all settled again, Elodie explains to the group that creative writing doesn't have to be fiction. We can use real experiences and emotions either alone or woven with our imagination into a story. She says it to everyone, but I'm certain it's directed to me more than the others.

I'd hidden a lot inside but, as I start to write, my emotions become distinct thoughts pouring onto the page. I describe the shock of becoming a single parent. The financial and practical difficulties and the loneliness that my growing son helped me through. How grateful I was for his easy-going nature, how much I loved him and how despite all that there was still something missing. Perhaps it was because we were so alike my son and I? I didn't actively look for someone else, but when I met Bill I didn't try very hard to resist the attraction I felt, and which he made clear was mutual.

Geraint had been hurt, but he'd not known how to show that other than through uncharacteristic anger. I saw later that he felt betrayed; that I was deserting him.

Our similarities, which had once made us close, pushed us apart. We knew just how to wound each other, we argued and said horrible things. I'm sure Geraint didn't mean them. I know I didn't. We were both too stubborn to admit our mistakes. He left and I haven't seen him since.

My piece ends with the fact that I've married Bill. Our marriage is good, but there's still something missing – my son. By the time I read it out, the individuals who'd started the course have become a group, eager to help and encourage each other.

I receive several good suggestions about things I could make clearer, what worked, how real it felt. I accept the words they intend as praise, rather than admit to being the woman who'd allowed the need for one kind of love to drive away the boy she cared for just as much, though in a different way.

There's time scheduled for questions at the end, but many of us are only half listening as we eagerly work on our writing. Some are still writing when a man starts stacking the vacated tables and chairs.

Eventually there are just the two of us. Elodie and I. We walk out together.

My daughter-in-law places a hand on my arm. "Margaret, would you like me to show it to him?"

"Do you think he'll read it?" I ask.

"Yes. I'm not sure, but I think so."

"Should I sign it or anything?"

"Perhaps put on your phone number?"

"Do you think he'll phone?"

She doesn't know of course, she's made that clear already. "All I can do is give him his tea, a chocolate wafer, and time. I hope he will."

Of course I hope so too, but more than that – I'm hopeful.

3. Mr Write

As soon as I saw him, I asked Sarah, the branch bitch, to watch the shop for a minute.

"Sure, Vera. No problem."

I think she'd noticed the arrival of one of our most regular customers too. Whether she realised my request was connected to that, I couldn't say. Her ready agreement almost certainly was. That's one reason I smoothed down my hair and applied fresh lipstick and got back behind the counter in double quick time. The other was of course that I wanted as much time within sight of him as possible.

Sarah had gone out to pretend to tidy the 'action' section, but unfortunately for her he opted for 'sci-fi' and made his choice too quickly for her to relocate.

His lovely dark eyes looked into my own as I served him. A piece of A4 paper was pushed across the counter at me. He smiled nervously as I unfolded it to read the few words typed in the centre.

Hello Vera I am gay. I would like too get too know some one enough to start a relationship but am too shy too ask any one out. That is why I am doing this in writing. What do you think?

This was followed by a big blob of biro that I could only assume was his signature. I read the note again slowly, trying not to show my disappointment as I struggled to find something to say. I had hoped that one of the reasons he often visited the video shop I work in was because he was interested in me. It appeared I was partly right – but I'd wanted to be his date not his dating agency. However I knew it must have been hard for him to open up to me like that and it showed he wasn't trying to hide anything. I was fairly new to the area and needed to make some friends and he seemed nice. I decided to make the best of an imperfect situation and offer my friendship.

"Why don't you take me for a drink after work and we can discuss it?" I suggested.

"Really? Oh wow! Yeah great," and he rushed towards the door. His enthusiastic response cheered me up. He might not fancy me but at least it sounded like he would appreciate my friendship.

He hadn't actually left the shop before came back. "Sorry, forgot to ask when you finish."

"We close at nine, I should be out about quarter past."

"Great, great. I'll be back," the last three words were said in a really bad Arnold Schwarzenegger impression. I shook my head wondering what I was getting into.

As soon as he'd gone, Sarah returned to the counter. "Ooh, he's gorgeous. It's only a matter of time before he's mine."

She knew I fancied him and couldn't resist having a dig at me whenever she could. It was on the tip of my tongue to tell her neither of us had a chance when I had a better idea.

"I don't think so, he's taking me out tonight."

Her bottom jaw dropped so low she looked like a snake about to swallow a medium sized animal.

I spent the rest of my shift with a permanent grin on my face. Some of it was just to annoy Sarah but I was genuinely looking forward to the evening. It was a change to be going out at all. Maybe he had some straight friends or a brother he would introduce me to. Sarah kept glaring at me, clearly jealous. She mellowed a bit though when she saw him waiting outside at ten to nine.

"Oh go on, get on out of my sight. I'll lock up tonight."

"Thanks, Sarah. I'll make it up to you."

"Too right you will," but she did manage a half smile as she said it. Maybe I would tell her the truth tomorrow. Perhaps we could become friends after all.

"Great, you're out early. Where would you like to go?" he said.

"Let's just go to The Bishop's Arms." I indicated the pub across the road.

"Great."

"Is that your favourite word?" I laughed

"Yeah, it's great! What would you like to drink?"

"White wine please." I found a couple of seats in a quiet corner and waited for my drink. "Thanks, that's great," I said when he brought it over.

"Watch it. That's my line!"

We both laughed but then neither of us could think of anything else to say. After a few minutes of silence I felt I should say something, however silly.

"My name is Vera, but of course you know that already." I point to the name badge I am wearing.

"Yes, I know but it's not because… There's something I have to tell you. I feel I can confide in you."

"Again! Go on what is it?"

"I'm dyslexic. I can't read or write very well, but I'm

getting better. I'm doing one of those courses you see advertised on the telly."

"Oh. How's it going?"

"Great! Seriously though I am improving and I've got a computer. That's good because it's easier for people to read than my dodgy handwriting and the spell checker is great."

I smiled at him; I could tell we'd get along well. He was so open and honest not to mention funny and really good looking. What a shame he didn't like girls. Apart from that he was perfect.

"Vera, what did you mean by again? I haven't made any other confessions."

"Your note."

"But that was just to ask you out and here you are, so I must have got that right."

Confused I took the sheet of paper from my pocket and asked him to read it to me.

He unfolded it and began. "Hi, I'm Gary …"

4. Coloured Vision

"I can't really give a man flowers, can I?" Denise asked as she spooned stew onto plates.

"Which man?" Christopher asked.

"You haven't been listening to a single word I've said, have you?" She added peas and carrots.

"Yes … something about your purse."

A single word was exactly accurate. As soon as Denise had mentioned her purse he'd thought she was the latest victim of the ginger-haired thief. The sight of the purse resting on their travel documents had quickly reassured him and he'd returned his attention to the latest crime-wave as his wife finished preparations for supper.

Christopher hoped to solve the case and show his superiors how right they'd been to promote him to detective sergeant. The thief, a short ginger-haired lad wearing a purple-hooded top, apparently managed to get the purses out of women's handbags or picked them up in shops while payments were made. He grabbed the cash and then dumped the purses. It seemed he worked very quickly as he didn't bother taking anything other than cash and he discarded the purses in busy public places almost immediately. Christopher knew that, because on several occasions the purses had been handed in to the bank before the owners had discovered they where missing.

"So, the flowers?" Denise prompted.

"Sorry, love."

"That's what I thought. I can't give a man flowers. A bottle of drink doesn't seem right either. Maybe money?"

"Is this for your bother's birthday?"

"No. For the man who found my purse. You were listening when I said I lost it and someone handed it into the police station?"

"Not properly," Christopher admitted. She had his attention now. "Have you cancelled the cards?"

"No need; they're all still here."

"A thief might have noted the numbers or something."

"Maybe, but there wasn't a thief. I do listen to you and there were no short, ginger-haired youths in town. I must have dropped my purse because I had it to pay for my shopping, but when I got to the bus stop, I couldn't find it. I went straight to the police station and it had already been handed in. Honestly it can't have been your thief, I still have all the money."

That didn't fit the usual pattern, but still … "I know it's unlikely, but just to set my mind at rest, please phone the bank."

When she'd done that, Denise asked how they had such a good description of the thief without the police having seen him.

"Witnesses. All the local stations have had reports from people who've seen the ginger-haired lad in his purple hoody looking shifty and then throwing something into flower beds, or under park benches. When they've gone to see what it was, they found the purses and handed them in."

"You should have said he had long hair. That should

make it easier to identify him."

"What makes you think he has long hair?" Christopher asked.

"If it could be seen with the hood up, it must be."

"Hmmm, good point. I'll check that. Now, what was that about flowers?"

"I thought I should reward the man who handed it in. If he hadn't, as well as losing the money which would have been bad enough, I'd have had to stop all my credit cards, changed my library ticket, get a new pass at work. I wouldn't have had much time to do all that before we went away. He's saved me a lot of effort although not as much as if I wasn't married to a paranoid copper."

"That's true. Sorry, but cancelling the bank cards is standard advice. Did you have much cash? Perhaps give him half as a reward for his honesty?"

"It was a lot. All in dollars; I'd just got the currency for our holiday."

"Maybe not half then." A thought occurred to him. "Did you have any British notes at all?"

"No, just dollars."

"Tell you what, don't worry about the reward. I'll get his address from the station, go and see him this evening and see he gets what he deserves."

The person who'd handed in Denise's purse, Mr Mills, had given his address as 47a St John's Close. When Christopher reached the cul-de-sac, he discovered it only contained twenty-six houses. He tried numbers seven and seventeen in case the officer on the desk had made a mistake, but at both he was told that the occupant had never heard of a Mr Mills.

Back at the station, Christopher looked up the details of wallets and purses handed in recently, paying particular attention to those who'd reported seeing the ginger-haired youth. He discovered that as well as Mr Mills, three different young women had made reports to the police. He checked the addresses they'd given and found out those didn't exist either. Christopher rang the two nearest police stations and discovered they'd also received visits from one man and three different young women who had apparently found purses dropped by the purple clad, ginger thief. Christopher made a few more enquiries and learned that all of the people who'd reported seeing the youth had given plausible sounding, yet non-existent addresses. Christopher knew that would be easy enough, as although a record was kept of people who handed in lost property, the people were not asked to prove their identity.

The following day, at his mum's house, Denise grumbled about the inconvenience of having no cards.

"I don't understand why you made her cancel the cards, love," Christopher's mum said to him.

Christopher tried to explain, but she cut him off. "I dropped my purse today, I suppose you think I should cancel mine, too?"

"I don't know. What happened?"

"I was in the café having a cup of tea and had to go to the lavatory. When I came back a youngster was holding out my purse. Said I dropped it when I stood up."

"Did he have long ginger hair?"

"No. She didn't. Pretty little thing, I tried to offer a reward, but she wouldn't hear of it."

'Pretty little thing' was a description he'd heard from two policemen when describing the young women who'd found purses. Possibly coincidence as there was more than one pretty girl in town, but Christopher was cautious.

"Sorry, Mum but I do think you should cancel your bank card."

Christopher visited the café and asked if they had CCTV. He was in luck; he watched the grainy time-lapse footage of his mother leaving her seat. A girl walked by the vacated table, bent down as though tying a shoelace right by his mother's bag then walked away. The girl disappeared for just over three minutes.

"She went outside, to have a cigarette, I suppose," the café owner informed Christopher.

The girl returned, just before his mum got back to the table, and could be seen returning the purse.

The girl's image was made available to all the local police stations. When she next handed in a lost purse, an officer followed her to a flat, which was then kept under surveillance. The other occupants of the property matched descriptions Christopher's colleagues had given for Mr Mills and the other two women who'd handed in purses and reported seeing a ginger thief.

Armed with a search warrant, Christopher entered their home and discovered a large quantity of cash and equipment for copying credit cards.

After the arrest, Christopher did eventually thank the man for handing in his wife's purse. "If you hadn't done that, I'd not have understood your clever ploy to make sure your victims didn't stop their credit and bank cards and I'd still be looking for a non existent ginger-haired thief."

5. A Strongly Worded Letter

Dorothy Jones settled herself in front of the TV, just as the presenter announced the next item would be, 'Willow, talking about letter writing'.

Lovely! Dorothy was a passionate letter writer and Willow was her favourite daytime TV presenter. Such a pretty girl, who spoke wonderfully clearly.

Dorothy had written to the production company when Willow first appeared on the show, to say how much she'd enjoyed listening to her. A good letter that; she'd managed to incorporate the word enunciation. At the time Willow was standing in for someone else, but she soon became permanent. Naturally Dorothy's letter wouldn't have been the whole reason for that, but surely it had helped?

The item on letter writing started well, describing missives by Queen Victoria, Jane Austen and Winston Churchill, which was all very interesting.

Then Willow said, "Because of texts and email, letter writing is now a thing of the past."

That wasn't right! Dorothy wrote letters all the time.

Dorothy enjoyed a regular correspondence with an old school friend and often wrote to the local newspaper. If a product was deficient in any way Dorothy wrote to the manufacturers with a complaint. If it exceeded her expectations she penned a testimonial. She'd recently written to the library complaining about the noise from the 'computers for beginners' class. Dorothy had made it clear the library was an unsuitable venue, as the raucous laughter which so frequently ensued was very distracting to anyone trying to concentrate.

Sometimes Dorothy wrote three letters a day. It took time to get them right. She looked up every long word in a dictionary to ensure she'd used it appropriately and spelled it correctly. Whenever she discovered a word which was particularly emphatic, or pleasing in any way, she made a careful note for future reference. It was worth the effort. Usually.

Her friend appreciated their shared correspondence and wrote back, often with amusing reminiscences from their time at school. The library though, had been rather cursory in their response. They'd replied 'the library is a place of education for all and it is our responsibility to provide services for the local community' in a manner which felt like an oft repeated stock response. The letter had ended by stating the writer would pass on Dorothy's concerns to the course facilitator.

He'd contacted her promptly, but that was the only aspect of the matter which met with Dorothy's approval. He was very dismissive, suggesting she either avoid the library on Thursday afternoons, or join in the fun, and enclosed a leaflet about the benefits of email! She'd been tempted to retaliate in strong terms, but refrained. She would confine her correspondence to areas where it was greeted with a modicum of respect.

Many of her letters received a fulsome apology, sometimes she also received vouchers for free or discounted products. Her opinions were frequently reproduced in the paper. Even those pointing out inaccuracies in reports were neatly printed above 'from

Miss D Jones, Highbank Avenue'. Validation, that was the term for it, not that Dorothy needed such a thing. What mattered was communicating with people, sharing memories and offering praise, or righting wrongs and correcting mistakes, as appropriate. Sadly the latter seemed to be required the most frequently.

Someone wrote in to the local paper about a reply they'd had from the local MP, noting that it was contradictory to the response Dorothy had obtained. 'It seems that with local elections coming up, they'll say whatever they think we want to hear.' Outraged at his betrayal of voters' trust, Dorothy had written to the MP accusing him of being sycophantic. An excellent word that.

The real trouble had started shortly before the European referendum. So much time was wasted discussing the issue when it was perfectly clear which way people should vote. Dorothy wrote to the paper to say so. It was a ludicrous to consider the alternative option, she pointed out. She was pleased with that; ludicrous was a word she'd been saving up for some time.

As anticipated, her missive was published. Excellent. Now people would see sense. But they didn't! There in black and white was a disagreement 'from Mr. R. Smith, sent by email'. He didn't just disagree but did so vehemently – a word she'd noted at the time of the scandal involving the mayor's daughter and been waiting to use ever since. Now she'd be unable to do so for fear it would be considered imitation.

Dorothy hurriedly penned a response, clarifying and expanding her position, and took it into the newspaper office so it could appear in the next issue. The girl on the desk suggested, again, that she email in her letters to save her the trouble. Dorothy didn't bother explaining, again, that she had no computer. It seemed no one took any notice of her unless she wrote down her words.

Dorothy's letter was indeed published, but she was horrified to see they'd printed 'effect' when the correct word was 'affect'. People would think the error was hers. Worse still was the remembrance that her draft was still in the waste paper basket, as that led to the mortifying realisation she'd made the error herself.

This was all the fault of that Mr R. Smith and his lamentable emails. Dorothy retrieved the copies of newspapers which contained her letters from the sideboard and scoured them for other comments from him. There were several, almost all disagreeing with what someone else had written in the previous edition. He seemed to delight in adopting a position of opposition. What an utterly disagreeable man.

She'd replied to his letter, taking him to task for making assumptions as to what would happen were Britain to leave the E.U. and pointing out that no one could predict the future. The following day his letter enquired as to whether she hadn't done the same thing. She hadn't of course. He was making a wild guess whereas she had described a self evident scenario. Even so Dorothy allowed that particular discussion to rest. To do otherwise might lend credence to his allegation.

For a time after that, Dorothy's letter writing experiences had been highly satisfactory. She contacted the council to express her appreciation of the flowers in the hanging baskets and tubs around town. They really brightened the area up and it seemed that her writing in to say so had also brightened the day of the workers who tended them.

Something else bright, which attracted Dorothy's attention, was a display of postcards in the Post Office. A bit cheeky they were, but fun. She'd bought one to send to her schoolfriend because they reminded her of those they used to laugh over at the seaside, and another to send to her great-niece, just because the cartoon featured someone with the same name. Felicity had sent a lovely letter back, thanking Dorothy for the card adding, 'I love it, Aunty. It's bang on trend – so retro!' Dorothy had chuckled over that and mentioned it in her next letter to her friend, saying the pair of them seemed to have been around so long they were almost back in fashion.

Unfortunately it wasn't long before Dorothy had occasion to write another letter of complaint, this time to an internet service provider. She also contacted the local newspaper to express her dismay about the noise and disruption caused by the digging up of her road to install internet cables, pointing out how little requirement there was for it in an area populated mostly by retired people.

Dorothy's nemesis, Mr R. Smith, replied, chastising her for her assumption older people were incapable of, or unwilling to, embrace modern technology. For many, he explained, it was a wonderful way of keeping in contact with family, of making new friends and sharing enjoyable experiences. He added that many pensioners were thoughtful, generous people who didn't object to something simply because it was of no direct benefit to themselves and would gladly put up with a little inconvenience if it benefitted others.

Naturally Dorothy replied, but she was so incensed by

his insinuation that she wasn't such a thoughtful person that it took her some time to compose a response which was both polite and legible. She arrived at the newspaper office just moments after it closed. That was on a Friday, so leaving the letter was pointless. It couldn't be used until Monday at the earliest and, as the men working on the road were already clearing up, would no longer be topical and therefore passed over.

Dorothy wrote to the paper concerning other issues. Every point she made was followed the very next day by a letter from Mr R. Smith refuting her carefully constructed points. It wasn't fair! He simply typed on a computer and emailed his thoughts in, whereas Dorothy had to create hers by hand and deliver them on foot.

Mr R. Smith and his negativity would not beat her! She would simply write letters expressing views to which no one could possibly object. For three days she wrote not a word. What did everyone like? What one thing could everyone agree upon?

Dorothy decided to listen to the conversations of others to assess their opinions. The tearooms in the High Street seemed the perfect location. The first conversation she overheard was between a group of four people who all agreed the candidate standing against the current MP was greatly to be admired. Perfect! Dorothy was sure nobody could fail to think that young woman would be an improvement on the current, sycophantic, incumbent.

The moment they'd left, a couple on the table next to Dorothy claimed the MP's rival was too inexperienced for the job, and expressed their support for an alternative candidate. Dorothy had to acknowledge that any letter on the subject of politics was unlikely to meet with unanimous agreement.

Over the next few days, and slices of cake, Dorothy heard that the fine weather was very welcome and that rain was needed, that a new television drama was superb and dreadful, that the NHS was useless and wonderful.

The tearoom customers couldn't even agree on their orders. Some favoured loose tea and others preferred bags. Half thought the jam should go on top of the cream on a scone and half were convinced the other way around was correct. They liked cupcakes best, or fruit loafs or tray-bakes.

As the waitress delivered a wedge of traditional sponge, Dorothy had her epiphany. She wrote to the paper praising the tearooms, its wide range of options which catered for those with different dietary requirements, and the way it encouraged friendly discussion.

Several people wrote in to express agreement – including Mr R. Smith. Dorothy had won!

For a few days, Dorothy had rested recumbent upon her metaphorical laurels. Then the young presenter Willow had stated, on national TV, that no one wrote letters now. Email was the thing. At first, Dorothy considered writing in to say how wrong that was. Then she decided that although it was an exaggeration to say no one wrote letters anymore, it did seem to be the case that email was becoming ever more popular. Dorothy grinned; if she could learn the techniques, she could send her carefully worded, grammatically correct, views via email. She'd be bang on trend – and totally retro!

At the library Dorothy enquired if there were space still available in the computing for beginners group. There was, at three every Thursday with Robert Smith. Dorothy was asked to arrive a little earlier for her first session so that Robert could have a chat with her to find out what experience she might have and to assess her needs.

Smith is a popular name, so it wasn't until Dorothy was actually talking to him and he showed her a letter he'd written to the paper and demonstrated how easily it could be submitted that she realised he was the Mr R. Smith she'd been communicating with for months.

Jones is also a popular name. He would not apprehend that she was the same Miss D. Jones with whom he'd frequently crossed adjectives and verbs, unless she told him. That was something she fully intended to do, but not until after the class. She would request he permit her to proffer her gratitude, for the computer tuition, at the tea rooms and then reveal the truth over a scone. Who knew, if he spread his jam on top of the cream, as was correct, perhaps they would become friends.

6. Private And Confidential

Jenny returned from running a work's training course absolutely shattered. All she wanted was to grab a snack from the fridge, have a quick shower, pull on comfy clothes and curl up with a good book. Chance would be a fine thing! When you share a home with three other women, getting a moment to yourself is rare. Jenny had understood that when she'd moved in.

What she hadn't realised was it wasn't just the space she'd be sharing, but every aspect of her life. She couldn't go anywhere, speak to anyone, do anything without them knowing. She was as likely to see her clothes on her friends' bodies as in her wardrobe. They used her towels and borrowed her make-up without stopping to wonder if she'd mind, let alone ask.

On the hall table was an interesting looking letter addressed to Jenny. She picked it up just as Moira opened the lounge door.

"Welcome back! Oh that's just news about your cousin's twins, plus photos of her and the kids," Moira said before Jenny noticed the envelope was slit open.

"Oh?"

"Er, yeah. I knew you were going to be on that course all week and thought it might be important. I looked so I could ring you if it was," she explained.

Jenny nearly told her not to interfere but remembered the time when she'd changed banks just before going on holiday and asked Moira to open the statement and check her wages had been paid in OK. They hadn't. Moira not only contacted Jenny's employers to get things sorted out but paid in some of her own money so Jenny didn't incur charges.

Biting her tongue, Jenny headed for the kitchen. There was a can of vegetable soup left in the cupboard from her last shopping trip. It was a bit bland but would do. Except she couldn't find it.

"Ros, have you seen my last can of soup?" she asked a girl bending over the oven.

"Thought you didn't like it." Ros sounded defensive.

"Not much but that's hardly the point. I'm hungry and it was mine!"

"Sheesh! Don't get your knickers in a twist, you can share my pie."

Jenny accepted a slice of cheese and leek flan. It was a lot tastier than her soup but she didn't give Ros the satisfaction of saying so.

Once she'd eaten, Jenny went up to the bathroom. She knew it was free as Sinead had just come down, wrapped in a towel and Jenny's dressing gown and smelling of something familiar. Sure enough the bathroom was a mess and Jenny's bottle of pricey conditioner was almost empty. By removing the top and adding a little water to rinse it out she just got enough to soften her curls.

After Jenny's shower she pulled on her jogging bottoms and favourite T-shirt. The outfit was almost as comfy as her dressing gown. She took down the empty conditioner bottle and chucked it noisily into the recycling bin. "Won't be buying that again, it doesn't last very long."

Sinaed's response was, "Ah, yes. Sorry I ran out of mine. That reminds me, I saw that mascara you said you couldn't get any more and bought you a couple."

"Right, thanks."

Telling herself they meant well and she was irritable because she was tired, Jenny went into the lounge intending to finish reading the book she'd forgotten to take away. Moira was curled on the sofa reading it.

She blew her nose. "This book is fab but when that little boy dies it's soooo sad. I never thought that would happen… oh." She flicked Jenny's bookmark. "Ooops. You hadn't got to that part."

"No, I hadn't."

"D'you want it back now?"

Jenny sighed. "It's OK. I'll just have an early night."

"Good idea, you've got an early start tomorrow."

"No, I'm having a lie in. You know I don't get many weekends off and …what?"

Moira indicated Jenny's phone. "You got a text when you were in the shower."

Jenny snatched up her phone and discovered Moira was right. Someone had gone sick and Jenny would need to spend the weekend preparing for, and travelling to, a course the following week in Southampton. As she typed and printed handouts, Jenny wished that shutting herself in her room working on her computer wasn't the only way for her to get any privacy. The thought gave her an idea.

Jenny, exhausted from the week and long train ride home, let herself into the house and saw a letter addressed to herself on the hall table. It had been opened. No surprise there.

No one appeared to admit to having read the letter. Jenny left it behind and went into the kitchen.

"Hi, Jen welcome back," Moira said. "You OK?"

"Yes fine. I'll just get myself something to eat." She opened the fridge door.

Jenny couldn't find the block of cheese she'd bought the previous weekend. Oh, there it was. She hadn't recognised it immediately as someone had tightly wrapped it in cling film for her. It didn't look as though they'd eaten even a tiny sliver. That was good. Unusual, but good.

When Jenny accepted Moira's offer of bread, instead of having the loaf chucked in her direction, two slices were extracted and put on a plate. "That enough or would you like a couple more?"

"That's plenty, thanks." Jenny made tea, toasted cheese sandwiches and cut them into quarters. Moira didn't help herself to a square or take a swig of Jenny's tea. Very odd.

After enjoying her snack Jenny went up for a shower. Her towels were neatly folded on the rail just as she'd left them on Sunday morning and none of her toiletries had mysteriously evaporated. The bathroom was sparklingly clean. Once showered Jenny was able to select from her entire clothes collection because everything was in her its proper place. This was beyond unusual.

She came downstairs again to discover her preferred spot on the sofa was vacant. Her favourite cushion rested there and her book awaited her on the coffee table. She read a couple of pages, then glanced up to see all three of her house-mates watching her.

"Um... you got a letter while you were away," Sinead

said.

"Oh?" Jenny put down the book and retrieved her letter. She returned to her spot on the sofa and removed the headed paper from the envelope, not mentioning it wasn't sealed.

The official sounding jargon informed the reader that Jenny's mild rash was impetigotaticeczemahyrditus, a very rare yet highly contagious skin complaint, which would flare up occasionally causing irritation, localised swelling and unsightly discolouration. As she read, Jenny scratched at her neck. The letter stated she mustn't share towels or clothing. Her make-up and hairbrushes should be used by her alone. Those people with cuts, scratches or sensitive skin would be well advised not to handle anything Jenny had touched.

"Girls, I have something to tell you," Jenny said.

"It's OK we already know," Ros admitted. "We'll take precautions."

"I hope it's not too sore?" Moira asked.

"No, not at the moment." Jenny couldn't resist scratching her calf as she answered.

"We'll leave you in peace then," Sinead said.

Jenny settled down to enjoy her book knowing that for a few weeks she'd have a little privacy and sole use of her own possessions. After that she'd be cured and things would go back to normal, at least until her condition flared up again. Or perhaps she could cure them of their bad habits by explaining why she'd faked the letter and made up the disease?

7. Writing George Off

I suppose it started when I saw the advert for a writing group. Saturday, I think it was or Sunday. No, not Sunday because I phoned and I wouldn't of called the library on Sunday. So it must of been the Saturday. Anyway, that's not really important.

I dialled and got that stupid press one for this and two for that thing. There wasn't a number to press for joining the writing group. There was one for giving up smoking. I nearly pressed that because listening to the robot phone woman made me stressed enough to want to smoke and the whole thing took long enough for me to get a habit and want to quit. Anyway, eventually I got through to someone who said to just come along to where it said in the paper at the time it said in the paper. Why the paper didn't just say come along was something she couldn't tell me.

When I told George about going to the group, he expostulated, "Writing? You?"

"It's what I said isn't it?" I demanded questioningly.

He shrugged. "They do say everyone has a book in them."

He'd have had one in him pretty sharpish except I hadn't finished reading it and wanted to know how it ended.

"Not everyone wants to write one," I contradicted. The money would be handy though. I could leave my rotten good for nothing waste of space husband for a start.

"Why join a writing group then?" he interrogated.

He never understands nothing George doesn't.

Anyway I joined the group. The leader woman, who looked a lot like a man, asked me if I'd brought anything to read. How daft is that?

"No. This is my first time here," I pointed out.

"And you've not written anything before?" inferred a woman who was obviously lesbian.

"No," I elucidated in the tone of voice I hoped would warn her not to start coming on to me.

"So what are you hoping to write and why?" demanded Blokey Leader Woman.

I hadn't expected the Spanish Inquisition. They advertised for new members then wondered why I'd turned up. This had to be harder work than actually writing!

Anyway this social worker type started talking and at least she seemed interested in me so I told her I had an unhappy life and a few people said I should get a hobby or something and I saw the advert in the paper.

"Writing can be very cathartic," Social Worker released.

Daft bat didn't seem to realise cathartic is something old people get wrong with their eyes. I didn't say anything though. She was trying to be nice so I didn't want to show her up.

Then everyone read stuff out. It was all a load of rubbish especially a poem by a complete tart. It didn't even rhyme but they all made a big fuss of her because she'd had stuff published. Reckon she'd lied to them about that because she didn't look rich and I'd never seen her on Celebrity Big Brother or nothing like that.

Anyway, after each person read we were supposed to say what we thought. Most people picked holes in things! What good was that? They'd better not do that when I write anything I thought. I wanted people to help me, not say it's no good. I said everything was nice. You'd think they'd of been grateful but they weren't.

The leader woman, her what looked like a man, said they'd like me to read something next time.

"Sure. I've got this fantastic book by Dan Brown," I enthused.

"I meant something written by you," she patronised.

"I don't know how, do I?" I complained. Come there to learn how hadn't I, but they were so busy telling each other where they'd gone wrong they didn't seem to have time to teach me nothing.

"How about a character sketch, Sandra, to get you started?" bloke woman exasperated.

"Sketch?" They wanted art now?

Social Worker, being dim herself, obviously felt sorry for me and explained. "A short description of someone, real or fictitious."

"OK," I acquiesced. If I described someone they didn't know they wouldn't be able to say it was wrong.

George was all sarcastic when I got home. "Written your masterpiece yet?"

I intimated, "I'm going to bed," in the same tone of voice as I'd used on the lesbian.

The next week, I read out my 'character sketch'. As I don't know any fictitious people I wrote it about George, but I didn't tell them that. I was just reminding them I was new to writing and explaining how I'd not had much time so they should make allowances when Tart walked in. Well, I say walked. Those shoes looked as though they were designed for her to spend the night on her back and I don't mean cause of falling over!

Anyway, I read. "He is called Arthur. He is five foot ten and a bit bald. He is annoying. He has brown eyes."

It took a while for anyone to say anything.

Leader Bloke/Woman spoke first. "It's quite short," she said diminutively.

"Yeah, well you said brief and like I said I didn't have much time." Was she deaf or what?

"It's not terribly descriptive," Tart criticised. "I couldn't really picture him. It could be one of many men."

Well, she would know.

"You really should try to show, not tell," Lesbian chipped in.

I'd show her something in a minute if she didn't stop smiling at me like that.

Social Worker got it. "Good start. We learn Arthur is fairly nondescript. The really interesting thing though is that he's annoying. I'd like to know more about his annoying habits."

So that week I wrote down everything annoying about George. I had to buy a new notebook.

Leader Woman didn't say it was short as she wasn't there. Or rather he wasn't. Turns out he's called Nigel and had a stomach bug which explains him looking like a man.

"That's so much better, I can really picture him now,"

Tart illuminated even though I hadn't written one word about how he looked.

"You were right about him being annoying and have showed it brilliantly," Lesbian soothed.

"I'd so like this to be turned into a story," Social Worker enthused. "For that you need a plot and for there to be a change." She rambled on a bit explaining what a plot was.

I got home later than expected, because I'd read for so long. Was George waiting up all concerned? No he was snoring his head off, just like I'd said on page 37.

Next time at the writing group, I read out a story where Arthur's poor wife killed him by putting something in his tea.

Tart investigated, "We really need to know what she gave him, if he'd taste it and if it would leave a trace."

I reckoned there would be plenty of things she could give a man that'd kill him without leaving a trace except a stupid smile on his face. Still, I could see she was trying to help.

When I got in, George queried, "How's your little hobby coming along?"

"Fine," I plotted. "I have to do some research though. Fancy a cuppa?"

Blithering idiot didn't notice the sleeping tablet I put in his tea. Well, he said it tasted funny, but he's always moaning about something. He didn't die, but I did think his snoring wasn't so loud that night.

At the next writer's meeting, I explained I'd researched the issue and still thought my 'character' would drink the tea.

"If he's like my husband he would," Lesbian prevaricated. "Give him a couple of gingernuts with it and he'd drink anything!"

Husband! He! Who was she trying to kid?

Nigel, whose stomach was better and who'd stopped pretending to be an ugly woman, interrupted, "If he was given enough to harm him he might notice."

That night I gave George two tablets. He didn't die, didn't even seem groggier than usual the next day, but definitely snored less.

I reported back to the group, "I'm confident in the method of murder, but want my 'viewpoint character' to get away with the crime. Do you have any suggestions for disposing of the body?" I entreated.

"Feed him to dogs," Tart gleefully suggested.

For a brief moment an image of her eating a small, wrinkled part of George's anatomy flashed through my mind.

The day after that I bought gingernuts and stepped up George's dose. He didn't suffer any ill effects and slept as quiet as a kitten.

By a stroke of luck, when I was in the doctors' getting my prescription renewed I overheard a woman with a bandaged leg saying she wasn't able to walk 'poor Snookums' and he was putting on weight. Quick as a sneeze, I said how much I liked dogs and offered to walk Snookums.

Next day I went to her bungalow and waited until she'd trudged to the door.

"Sandra, how kind of you to do this," she gratified.

There was something wriggling on her elbow.

"He's a Pomeranian," she yapped. Pomeranian is clearly a synonym for 'most hideous and stupidly small dog in the world ever'. It looked like I'd have to slice George very thinly.

I also needed to make room in the freezer for most of him so decided to throw a barbecue. Naturally I invited my friends from the writing group.

Tart was first to arrive. I'd assured her there was no dress code. She'd taken that as an excuse not to get dressed. I could see more body piercings than clothing and noticed George's tongue hanging out.

Nigel raved to George, "Sandra's a wonderful writer!"

"Certainly tells me some tales," George patronised dismissively.

"She's improved so much that I've decided to put her wonderful crime story into our next anthology," Nigel announced alarmingly.

With my confession about to be printed, I thanked good karma I hadn't already poisoned George.

"What's the point?" George scoffed. "You won't make any money."

"I will, but actually I don't need to," Nigel enlightened. "I run a profitable publishing company. I'm so looking forward to making Sandra's growing talent available to the reading public."

I think I'd already mentioned Nigel looked very manly, but I hadn't until then realised how attractive he was. Neither had I realised how attracted he was to me. Yippee.

Anyway, one year on and we're at another party. It's the Christening of Not Lesbian and her husband's twin girls.

The pair of them are carrying on like they're already working on having a boy next time.

I'm there with my new husband, Nigel. (Yes, reader - I married him!) Tart's with her new man; George. (After I'd divorced him she got what she could out of him until the snoring drove her mad, then she too dumped the useless excuse for a human being. I don't hold a grudge – she's always very helpful to me in the writing group.)

Social Worker did say Nigel's publishing company was a deus ex machina. She's probably right, but at least this isn't one of those times where I wake up and find out it was all a dream.

8. The Subtle Art Of Communication

"Don't take too much notice of what she says," Connor warned just before Beverly met his mother.

Martha had been lovely though. They'd met in a tea room and she'd insisted on treating them. "You can't beat a nice cup of tea," she'd said, quite loudly. "Especially if there's plenty of milk. I always tip better if there's plenty of milk."

The waitress, who'd been close by at the time, soon returned with a second jug of milk.

A few days after Connor proposed, Beverly noticed Martha in the post office. She'd heard her first, telling the cashier the letter she was sending contained wonderful news.

"My son is about to marry a lovely girl."

When Martha joined Beverly she pointed to a man not three feet away. "It's his wife's birthday next week. I hope he remembers this time, she was ever so disappointed last year."

Beverly and Connor visited Martha regularly after their wedding. Once, as she let them in, she'd said, "How thoughtful of you to visit me so often. It means such a lot."

When they'd gone into the lounge they saw Connor's brother was making a rare visit. He'd clearly heard every word. Beverly guessed Martha had meant him to.

Martha frequently shouted into her mobile phone, accidentally sent texts or emails to the wrong people and forgot who was in earshot. She claimed modern technology confused her and she was getting absent minded, but Beverly wasn't convinced. That's why the next few things she overheard hurt so much.

"… modern career women. Do you think my Connor's girl will expect to keep that fancy job of hers when she has children?" reached her as she walked down the side of Martha's in response to the 'I'm in the garden' note. Another time Martha answered a call from a friend. She left the room but didn't close the door properly so they caught all her moans about how Connor would be expected to keep 'that Beverly' when she had children.

"It's not fair," Beverly said once Martha had gone. "I can't win. Either I'm a career woman who'll neglect our children or I'm a gold digger who wants you to support me."

"I'm sure she doesn't really think either of those things."

"Maybe not, but as she never says anything to my face it's hard to tell, and if I tackle her I'll just seem like an eavesdropper."

"I reckon she's just looking forward to having grandchildren and it's her way of letting us know."

"She's a bit premature. It's not as though we've discussed ourselves what we'll do when we have children."

"Maybe we should?"

By the time Beverly was expecting their first child they'd agreed she'd give up work and calculated they could, just, afford that.

Once Martha learned of the pregnancy, Beverly heard her mother-in-law mention the forthcoming child on numerous occasions. Every word was positive.

Martha accidentally sent Beverly a copy of an email, addressed to a friend, expressing the hope that she'd be allowed to babysit frequently and asking 'do you think they'll be offended if I offer to pay for having the nursery decorated?'

Beverly called her mother-in-law to say she'd seen the message.

"I can't think how I managed to send it to you."

"Don't worry about it. And don't worry about offering your help, I'll be pleased to have it before and after the baby is born."

"Thank you, Beverly dear. I will try not to interfere too much, but promise you'll say if I do."

"OK then." Beverly wasn't sure she'd dare… unless she said it to someone else in Martha's hearing?

Everything went well until two months before the birth. Connor became moody. He worked late, left the room when he got a phone call and once called 'Rachel' in his sleep. There was a pretty redhead in his office called Rachel. A coincidence?

Beverly visited Martha. She couldn't actually voice her concerns, especially as she could easily be wrong, but she dropped a few hints about his long hours. Although she overheard several of Martha's conversations over the next few days, Beverly heard nothing to either confirm or allay her fears.

Then Martha called Beverly at work. "I'm going into town to look at a few things for the baby. Can you meet me for lunch?"

"That would be lovely."

Beverly crossed the crowded restaurant, half expecting her mother-in-law to be on the phone.

"You're looking tired dear, is everything OK?"

"I'm fine," Beverly said.

"Good. Pregnancy has funny effects on people. Makes them do the silliest things."

Was she trying to say Beverly had imagined Connor was behaving oddly? "I have been feeling a bit emotional," she admitted. Perhaps Martha would reassure her?

"I hadn't noticed, love."

That wasn't reassuring at all.

Martha chatted throughout the meal telling Beverly how much she was looking forward to being a grandmother, what wonderful parents she and Connor would make and what a good, loving wife he had.

Beverly guessed Martha was trying to say that even if Connor had behaved badly it was just a temporary blip and was asking Beverly to forgive him. Of course few mothers, particularly not Martha, were likely to come straight out and say they thought their son capable of an affair.

That evening Beverly told Connor she'd had lunch with his mother. "We went to Luigi's. That's near your office, isn't it?"

"Yes, why?"

"I just wondered if you heard her. She spoke loudly."

"We didn't …um, I… What did she say?"

"Stuff about people doing silly things and how much you're looking forward to having a child and what a good marriage we have."

"She's right. I'm looking forward to our baby being born and I love you." He held her as close as her bump allowed. "I won't be working late anymore."

"That's good news."

Later Connor went out into the garden and made a phone call.

Beverly didn't know if he left the patio doors open on purpose, but a few phrases reached her, "all over," "nearly made a terrible mistake," and "I love my wife."

9. Words In German

You know that thing where you don't realise you want something until someone else has it? Shoes you weren't sure about look perfect when another woman buys the last pair in your size, and an empty supermarket shelf makes you crave whatever it held… There's probably a special word for it in German. The German's have lots of good words we don't. *Schadenfreude* for example. It means taking pleasure in another's misfortune. Not that I often do. I don't begrudge the Germans their language either; what's good enough for Shakespeare and the Queen is good enough for me.

I don't usually want what other people have, but I know someone who does. The first time I really noticed it I was nine. School friends and I were taken to a restaurant for my birthday meal. Probably nowhere fancy, but it seemed so at the time. For dessert my friend Paige ordered something chocolatey. I opted for trifle. Hers was on a regular plate, served with a blob of ice cream and dusted with cocoa. Mine was in a huge glass, topped with masses of whipped cream, and sauce which dribbled down the sides. There were wafers and cherries and spirally bits of chocolate. Immediately Paige wanted it. She looked so disappointed in her choice that I swapped to cheer her up.

Now that sort of thing is OK if the other person is your friend and you get something good in exchange… But not long afterwards I was at Paige's birthday party. It was held in a burger place and we could choose what we wanted. Again Paige wanted what I'd ordered. It was her birthday, so I agreed. No big deal.

It mattered slightly more when we got older. Two days after I lost my favourite sweater she was wearing an identical one, which she claimed she'd bought the previous week. And she copied my hairstyle. People referred to her as my *doppelgänger*. They said imitation was a form of flattery. I was less polite, but only in my head.

Later she wanted my boyfriend and took him away from me. I was heartbroken in that short-lived but all consuming way you are at sixteen. Then I realised that if Paige could take him so easily he wasn't much good. Something that was proved when he dumped her for a younger model. But I'm getting ahead of myself.

Another time she and her husband wanted the house me and mine were looking at and put in an offer over the asking price. Is *gazump* a German word? It sounds as though it should be.

You're probably thinking she wasn't much of a friend and I agree with you. Being around her caused me a great deal of angst. If I could have done, I'd have avoided her completely, but I couldn't. Even worse, I had to be polite. By then we worked at the same place and the management were very keen on teamwork and everyone getting along. I'm a team player, something I was hoping would be recognised and rewarded.

Paige, as you might have imagined, wasn't so keen on the sharing of ideas for the good of all, especially when it came to promotion opportunities. A new department was to be opened in Germany and there were three of us in with a chance of being selected to run it. The management decided that, rather than have us compete directly in interviews, we'd each be invited to submit a proposal for improving performance in any area of the company's business and the best would be offered the post.

"I'm not sure I want it," I said when I knew Paige could hear. "I'm really struggling to learn the language. I thought French was bad enough with masculine and feminine words, but the Germans have neutral as well."

"You've been learning German?" Paige asked.

"Umm, no. Well, just a few key phrases. You know, so I can be polite to our new colleagues."

She didn't believe me. Maybe it was because she saw how hard I worked on my proposal. We all worked hard, but separately.

"The company like teamwork. We've been friends for so long," Paige said, "Let's put that to use and increase our chances."

She was wrong about us being friends, but otherwise had a point. Working together would put us ahead of the other contender. I let her talk me into it. We both offered each other suggestions, and read through the documents to check for silly spelling mistakes and that sort of thing. To help with this, we used the internal file sharing system. Somehow my brilliant proposal ended up being submitted under Paige's name from her computer and hers was sent in as though it was my work. To be fair hers was pretty good too, it just wasn't as brave as mine, nor as wide ranging in scope. It was safe.

"We can't tell them it's a mix up," Paige said. "We'll look incompetent."

She sort of had a point there too. I wasn't convinced for a moment that it was an innocent accident. However, if I'd said so, either I'd reveal myself as someone who let my work be stolen, or it would seem I was lying in order to take credit for her work and land her in trouble.

The proposal I'd worked so hard on, and which she'd submitted, was for the German office. Thanks to my efforts, Paige got the job. For months beforehand she had intensive German lessons. That's when her husband started his affair. That's the husband who'd once been my boyfriend. He eventually left her for the pretty young thing he met as she was learning the difference between *guten Morgen mein Herr* and *guten Tag gnädige Frau*. No, I wasn't terribly sympathetic.

The ambitious development plan she'd submitted was risky. Riskier than she or the management had fully realised. Paige was unable to make it work. Flaws in her calculations were revealed. Flaws she should have spotted. Indeed probably would have spotted had she made them, not just stolen them from me. Are you thinking I was careless? Paige probably is, but then she probably doesn't realise I only pretended to want the job so she'd take it.

She lost her promotion. Alone she couldn't meet the mortgage payments and lost her house. You know, the one she'd paid over the odds for just so I didn't get it.

So now she's back and wanting her old job. She can't have that as it's been filled. Mine is vacant as I'm now part of the management. The management who likes team players, not those who take what they want from others, so I think she'll be out of luck. Which brings us right back to were we started; *schadenfreude*.

10. The Greengrocer's Apostrophe

Barbara scowled at the greengrocer's shop. She had no fruit at home, but she wasn't sure she could go in there again. No, that wasn't the problem exactly. She could go in all right, but she wouldn't be able to simply buy a bag of nice crisp apples and walk out again, not without saying something.

"You don't know what you're doing with your apostrophes!" was what she wanted to say. No one would take any notice, even if she said it very loudly, which is exactly what she did want to do.

It didn't seem to be bothering anyone else. Nobody but retired schoolteachers seemed the slightest bit interested in correct grammar and punctuation these days. Barbara knew that if she were to go over and put him right, most people would think she was making a fuss over nothing.

To give him his due, Craig, the young man who owned the shop, was polite and cheerful and gave the correct change without having to rely on the till or a calculator. He spelled the names of all his wares correctly. No trouble with broccoli, or collie instead of cauliflower or extra Ns in banana, but still…

The fruit and vegetables were always good quality and displayed in such an enticing manner that even young children pointed to items they'd like their mothers to buy. Even some older kids shunned the offerings of the sweet shop in favour of oranges or grapes. That was a good thing, but still…

On each of the neatly handwritten signs was an unnecessary piece of punctuation. Craig advertised plum's, carrot's and pumpkin's. Whenever there was an s at the end, he'd slipped in an entirely erroneous apostrophe. Surely the signs hadn't always been like that and Barbara had failed to notice? That thought was possibly the most unsettling of all.

As Barbara continued to observe the shop a young woman stopped outside, examined the window display and shook her head. For a moment it seemed she'd go in, and Barbara was sure it wouldn't be to make a purchase, but she turned and retraced her steps.

Barbara could stand it no longer and crossed over the street. She let herself into the shop, snatched up a sign saying apricot's and took it to the counter.

"Good afternoon, Mrs Ashe. I haven't seen you for a while. How can I help you?" Craig asked.

"I've come to help you, though I don't suppose you'll see it that way." She proceeded to explain that apostrophe s was used to show possession and that for plural the letter s alone was sufficient.

"Except with potatoes and tomatoes, then an e is needed as well," Mr Ashe said.

"Er, well yes, that's true, but my point is that …"

"Apostrophe s is possessive. It shows that something belongs to or is a property of that item or person?" He took a pen and added words until the sign read, 'the apricot's scent is deliciously aromatic'.

"Er, yes. Exactly like that." She took the sign from him and carefully replaced it. As she did so, the scent reached her nose and it was exactly as he'd described it. "I'll take a pound of these, please."

The encounter had wiped all thought of apples from Barbara's mind, so she returned to Craig's shop the next day. The extended sign for apricots was still written correctly. All around it were others reading, apple's, peach's and plum's.

"You've used a possessive apostrophe incorrectly again," she told him.

Craig selected a sign and amended it to read, the 'peach's juice is very sweet'. "It really is you know, can I tempt you to a couple?"

"Yes, all right."

The pattern continued for days. Often Barbara saw the same young woman shaking her head despairingly at the shop window. Whether that were the case or not, Barbara would go in, see another incorrect sign and end up buying some kind of fruit, but never apples.

After being persuaded to try lychees, Barbara finally asked, "If you know the signs are wrong, why do it? Admittedly you've somehow tricked me into spending much more here than I used to, but it can't really bring in much extra custom. Sadly only retired teachers are likely to even notice."

"Sadly you seem to be right, but I'm still hopeful you're not quite correct."

Before she could ask him what he meant there was a clatter as several boys leaned their bikes against the shop window. One of the lads charged in. "Uncle Craig, I'm starving. Can I have a banana, please?"

"Have you done your homework?"

"Yes."

"Spellings then… Come on."

The boy gave a list of items commonly found in a kitchen and spelled most of them correctly. When he added an extra l to colander, Craig invited him to try again. The boy got it right at the second attempt and then gave two more correct answers. The last word was potatoes, which he also got right.

"And in potatoes, is there any punctuation?"

The boy grinned. "An apostrophe!"

Barbara tried to speak, but no words came.

"Good lad." Craig gave the boy a whole hand of bananas. "Share them with your mates."

"You're setting a bad example for him," Barbara finally managed to say.

"Fruit is healthy."

"That's not what I mean, as I'm sure you know."

"I do, but… Look, I'm a greengrocer… It's hard to explain, but I am sorry I'm upsetting you."

Craig looked like he meant it. He even gave her a free orange by way of apology. Barbara took that and the punnet of strawberries she couldn't resist, despite them being labelled strawberry's. This was all so odd. Craig was obviously clever enough not to make the same mistake over and over. He seemed far too kind to be deliberately tormenting her, so why did he keep doing it?

She got her answer the next Saturday. As she was paying for a bag of nice crisp apples a young woman came in. The same one Barbara had seen outside the shop shaking her head.

"I can't stand it any longer!" she said, waving the avocado's sign and confirming Barbara's suspicions. "It doesn't just annoy me but it's leading my pupils astray. One lad today said I must be wrong as the greengrocer does it like that and he's really smart as he has his own business. He also told me you're not married. I don't know what's going on, but it has to stop."

"I'm really sorry," Craig said and again he sounded it. "If both I and my nephew stop putting apostrophes where they're not supposed to be, will you come out to dinner with me?"

"Dinner?"

"A meal, eaten in the evenings. Dinner is the noun, to dine would be the verb. Go on, say yes. I'll bring a red pen and you can correct the menu if it needs it."

"I really don't know what to say," the young woman said.

"I do," Barbara said. "Say yes." Then added very quietly to Craig, "You certainly know what you're doing with your apostrophes." She left with apples and a smile on her face.

11. Lucky Escape In High Street Incident

"Hi, Kerry," Rod called as he let himself in.

She tried to stifle her annoyance. Technically it was his house as much as hers, despite their separation.

He'd called out to her, just as he always had. As though she'd be pleased at his arrival. At one time she would have been. Not so long ago the sound of her husband's voice, sight of his smile or warmth of his hug had made all her problems disappear and turned the world into a wonderful place. It was hard now to remember that she'd ever been happy about anything.

"Kerry?" Rod stuck his head into the front room. "I've got your shopping."

She had accepted his offer to bring her some groceries; it was the least he could do after nagging her for living off take-aways and chocolate. She knew it wasn't healthy, but with a broken wrist she shouldn't be blamed for taking the easiest option. If he wanted gratitude, he'd come to the wrong place. Or at the wrong time.

When Rod had called round earlier to see if she needed anything, he'd left a copy of the local paper. Daytime TV had long since lost the little novelty it had possessed when she'd first had time to watch. Nothing held her attention these days. Kerry had skimmed through the paper, not taking anything in until she saw her own name.

The article was titled 'Lucky Escape in High Street Incident'. It made no sense to Kerry. Why mention the

High Street when she'd been nowhere near that part of town? As for luck, the only sort she had was the bad kind, such as some thug pushing her over. There was a picture of him. She remembered his face looming over her as she'd lain in agony on the cold, hard pavement. The report claimed he was a hero!

Kerry threw the paper aside. Needles of pain shot up her arm, causing anger at her attacker to turn to fury. It hadn't been a good moment for Rod to return.

She heard him messing about in the kitchen, then he appeared with a carrier bag, containing what looked like apples.

"Is that it? You said I need proper food and I just get apples."

He took a breath and spoke slowly and calmly as though trying to pacify a child. "I've put milk, eggs, cheese and lots of salad in the fridge. All nutritious stuff which is easy to prepare."

"There's no need to patronise me. It's bad enough some idiot broke my wrist without that!"

"That's not fair," Rod said.

He was right. She shouldn't have snapped at him. "I'm bored stuck in on my own with nothing to do." As she said it she knew what she'd intended as an explanation came out as another complaint. She was on her own because she'd told him to go and stay with his mother. Kerry had thought he was making her miserable, but soon realised she was at least as unhappy on her own.

"I can't win," Rod said. "Yesterday you were annoyed when I suggested we go for a walk. Today you're annoyed because you're staying in all the time."

Kerry hadn't been annoyed at the suggestion of the walk so much as the way he'd said it. That even if she did feel uncomfortable, the exercise would be good for her. It had reminded her of the office manager suggesting she accept a job share as though he was doing her a favour by cutting her hours and pay in half. Nothing had gone right since then.

Rod had claimed to be worried about her, saying he thought she was depressed. She'd kicked him out, so at least she didn't have to put up with his smug expression when she made an appointment at the doctor's, or listen to his 'I told you so' when she came home with leaflets and a prescription. Well, he was wrong, she'd been taking them for a month and they weren't helping at all. Just an excuse to fleece her for the prescription charge, they were. She was only still taking them because it seemed the easiest disposal method.

"Anything else I can help you with, before I go?" Rod asked.

"No."

Kerry cried once he'd left. He'd been trying to be kind, just as he always had. She'd meant to apologise for her grumpiness and thank him for going shopping and she'd just got angry again. She couldn't understand why he kept coming back when all she did was moan.

Her thoughts tumbled round in her head. Nothing made sense. Was she going mad? The doctor had said depression made it difficult to concentrate and remember details. Maybe he, and Rod, were right to say that's what was wrong with her. She hoped so, because that might mean the medication and advice she'd been given could help. Hope! That word hadn't entered her thoughts for too long.

If she read the article slowly, perhaps she could work out what had really happened to her. Carefully Kerry retrieved the paper. She learned the man she'd thought had attacked her had seen her step off the kerb, without looking, straight in front of a bus. He'd thrown himself at Kerry in order to knock her onto the relative safety of the pavement. Oh! She remembered; she'd been upset Rod had left her and intended to visit the church where they'd married.

She *had* been where the report said she was. The man who pushed her *was* a hero. Maybe it wasn't only his motivation she'd misjudged? Her boss said the company was going through a rough patch and he had to cut costs, which meant cutting staff. Perhaps he really had suggested the job share not because he wanted to get rid of her, but because he didn't.

And Rod. He'd been so kind to her since she'd broken her wrist. Tears spilled down Kerry's face as she remembered all he'd tried to do for her before that. Attempting to persuade her to eat well, take exercise, contact friends she'd lost touch with. To fill the time she no longer spent at work in doing things she enjoyed rather than slumped in front of the TV feeling sorry for herself. He hadn't been able to pull her out of the dark hole she was hiding in, but that wasn't his fault.

Kerry read the rest of the article. There were such lovely comments from Rod saying how grateful he was that she was going to be OK. He thanked her rescuer and the hospital staff who'd cared for her. There wasn't one mention of any rows or complaints from Kerry. Instead he'd described her as the happy woman she'd once been and said how much he was looking forward to her recovery. It wasn't just her wrist he was thinking of, though no one but the two of them was likely to realise that.

Kerry reached for her phone and called Rod.

"Are you OK?" Rod asked.

"I read the article in the paper. I didn't know about the bus. I thought he just pushed me. I've been wrong about a lot of things."

"You've not been well." His tone was cautious.

"Yes, and without that young man's quick thinking I could be dead. I should thank him. And you. Will you come home, so I can try?"

"I'm on my way."

12. Not So Angelic Angie

Once again Angela experienced that feeling of everything being too good to be true. Not long ago she'd been the least popular girl in her class and wretchedly miserable. Now she was stood beside a wonderful man who loved her, surrounded by friends and family wishing her well. She was blissfully happy, or would be if she could convince herself she came close to deserving to have Iain in her life.

As she glanced round the crowded bar she spotted a face which looked familiar. It couldn't really be Becky from school though. They'd not run into each other since they'd left nearly six years ago and it wasn't at all likely the other girl would be eager to offer Angela her congratulations. They'd not exactly been friends. School bullies don't have real friends.

"You OK, love?" Iain asked.

"Of course!" She plastered on a smile suitable for a girl enjoying her engagement party. "Um, do you know that girl over there?"

"Which one?"

"In the rather… unusual blue dress." Angela felt secretly pleased with her tactful description. Someone less kind might have mentioned how unfashionable it was, or compared it unfavourably with the much more casual outfits worn by most other guests. It was quirky, glamorous and suited the wearer.

"Oh, that's my cousin Becky. Nice girl, I'm sure you'll get on."

That seemed highly unlikely. For some inexplicable reason, Iain adored Angie and saw her as kind, caring and quietly confident. Thanks to him she'd become like that. Or at least a lot more like that than she used to be.

Iain must have picked up something wasn't quite right. "Do you know her?"

"Not really. It was a long time ago."

Iain would be horrified at what she'd put Becky through. Somehow she had to stop him finding out. Angela considered trying to avoid Becky all evening, but that would just delay the inevitable.

"I'm just going to the ladies," she said and slipped away.

Angela's Dad was in the army and they'd moved around a lot. They stayed long enough in Germany for her to pick up an accent, but otherwise she'd always been the new girl. The one who sounded funny and didn't know the cool places to hang out. She had no friends or mother to talk through the issues of puberty, boys and clothes. Her insecurities had taken the form of lashing out at everyone else. Rather than risk discovering the others didn't like her much, she'd taken control of the situation and made sure they didn't.

Angela didn't resort to violence; she didn't need to. Her jibes and insults were generally enough to ensure she was left alone. It hadn't worked with Becky who'd suffered from eczema. A kind person would have sympathised with the flaky skin and daubs of ointment. Angela nicknamed her Flecky Becky.

Instead of retaliating by calling her Acid Angela, or adapting Angela's surname of Bugley as the other kids had, Becky called her Angelic Angie. A more secure girl might have stopped to wonder if that could be because of her long blonde hair, huge blue eyes and sweet, clear singing voice. Angela had assumed it was an attack and defended herself the only way she knew how; with insults. When those ran out she'd whispered, "You hurt my eyes, Flecky Becky. Get out of my sight."

One time she'd seen Becky talking to a boy she liked and thought of ridiculing her in front of him. Before she'd decided whether to or not, the boy walked off and her chance had gone.

Becky could so easily do that to her now. No, it wouldn't be the same kind of thing at all. All Becky would have to do was tell the truth, or even a quarter of it, and Iain would see what kind of girl his fiancée was and dump her.

One of Angela's colleagues was in the bathroom, touching up her make-up. Angela could have done without her right then. Helen was hard work. Some people called her Hell and Angela could see why, but it would have been horribly rude not to invite her along with everyone else.

"Not a bad party, Angie," she said.

Angela gritted her teeth and thanked her. She still hated that nickname and had twice asked Helen not to use it.

"Nice shoes," Angela said. They weren't especially nice, but they were much higher than the ones she wore for work and the only part of her outfit which was at all dressy. If she was going to attempt to talk Becky round, it might be a good idea to practise a bit of flattery.

"Fab, aren't they? Not like those horrible sandal things the girl in the ghastly blue dress is wearing. Who is she anyway?"

"My fiancé's cousin."

"Oh god, you won't have to have her as a bridesmaid, will you?"

"Not have to, no." It was extremely doubtful Becky would want that role, but Angie would be delighted to give it to her if she did. She'd be willing to do just about anything to show Becky she was a better person than she'd been at school.

"Don't tell me you're considering it, Angie. I know that type and she'd ruin your wedding."

"Really?" It seemed far more likely she'd stop it happening.

"Make a fool of herself trying to catch your bouquet, dance with smelly old uncles and sticky kids like a complete loser. She'll probably get drunk and be rude or sick. I've already had to give her a hint about all those snacks she was stuffing in her mouth earlier and how sparkly outfits don't work on a fuller figure. Angie, let me tell you …"

It was like listening to echoes of her schoolgirl self.

"No, Helen. Let me tell you something. First off, Becky is actually a nice person. Much nicer than either of us. Second, she looks great and is one of the few who bothered to get dressed up for my party. She isn't fat, but even if she was that would be no excuse for a stranger to comment on her eating habits. Third, I really hope people of all ages forget to be self conscious and have fun dancing at my wedding even if it's uncool. Fourth, don't ever call me Angie again. Fifth, get out of my sight."

Angela shut herself in a cubicle and sat on the toilet seat taking steadying breaths. She needed a few more when she realised there was someone in another cubicle. How long had they been there? Perhaps they weren't one of her guests. Angela had spoken to Helen in an angry hiss rather than a yell, so perhaps she hadn't been overheard. It was all wishful thinking, but possible. She waited until she was sure the other person had left, then went in search of Becky.

Fortunately she found her alone. Angela apologised to Becky and did her best to explain the reasons for her past behaviour. She begged not to say anything to Iain and apologised again.

"Do you really think any of that matters?" Becky asked.

"I know it's no excuse, but I've changed. Honestly I have."

"Oh? You're not insecure now then?"

"Not when I'm with Iain. He makes me a better person and I really do love him. Please, Becky, don't make me lose him. I'll do anything you want."

"There you are!" It was Iain. "Becky, Angela says she knows you, but she's making a mystery out of it. Come on, spill the beans."

"It's no mystery," Angela said. "We went to school together."

"Old school friends! Why ever didn't you say? Does Becky know some deep dark secrets?"

"Remember me telling you how I used to get called Flecky Becky?" Becky said.

"I do, yes."

Angela felt sick.

"One of the kids who did it was known as Angie. Either Acid Angie or Angelic Angie depending on whether or not the other person was trying to make friends."

"I can't see why anyone would have wanted to make friends with her," Iain said.

Angela could only agree with him.

"I see why you hate being called Angie too, love," Iain added.

Becky took a deep breath. "It took her a while, but our Angela here got rid of Acid Angie."

"Wow! That's amazing!" Iain said and kissed her cheek.

"Not really," Angela said. "I just made her see how hurtful she'd been and promise she'd never, ever do it again."

"I'd say that was amazing. Oh sorry, my brother is signalling. I'd better see what he wants."

Once he'd gone Angela said, "Thank you."

"You know you said you'd do anything I wanted?"

"Yes."

"When you throw the bouquet, aim it in my direction will you? I want to catch it, but preferably without making too much of a fool of myself."

"You heard?"

Becky winked. "Not a word, but I will tell you something. If you arrange for me to sit next to the gorgeous bloke Iain has picked as his best man I promise I'll never, ever call you Angie again."

13. The Sharing Of Information

As Arne was leaving the bowls club grounds, a friend called him back.

"Are you all right for a lift to the match tomorrow?" Martin asked.

"Yes, thanks mate. Greg is going to drive, so I'll go with him."

"Are you sure that's a good idea?"

That seemed a strange thing to ask. Greg was on their team and lived next door to Arne. He seemed the perfect choice. OK, he was a bit dull and never talked about anything except his health or sport, but as they'd be travelling to a match Arne thought he'd be able to keep him to the subject that interested him.

"Old Greg is OK," Arne said.

"Well I wouldn't want to be driven around by an alcoholic."

"Alcoholic? Greg? I've never seen him drink anything stronger than Diet Coke."

"You don't with alkies do you? They drink in secret."

"So because you've never seen him drink, you've decided he's an alcoholic?"

Martin was known for getting the wrong end of the stick, but even so, Arne thought he'd put two and two together and got eight.

"No, Arne; it's not just because of that. He's been looking kind of yellow lately and he told me about some test he's got to have done on his liver. It's obvious, isn't it?"

Not to Arne it wasn't.

He was thinking about what Martin had said as he walked home, which is why he almost missed seeing Greg in the street outside their houses. He was taking out the recycling bin and by the way he was struggling Arne guessed it was pretty full.

"Evening Greg," he said.

Greg jumped; either he hadn't seen Arne or he was feeling guilty about something. Arne couldn't help wondering if the bin was heavy because it was full of empty whisky bottles.

"Evening, Arne. I wasn't expecting to see you this early,' Greg said.

Arne wasn't sure if it was just due to the street lights, but he did look very yellow.

"Didn't want to drink too much the night before a big match," Arne said.

"Very sensible, we'll all want to be clear headed if we're to have a hope of beating the Aldershot Avengers."

Arne went inside, hoping Greg would take his own advice. He tried to get Katie to tell me what was up with Greg. She worked at the health centre, so she should know.

"You know I can't discuss any of the patients," Katie said.

"Yes, but he's driving me to the match tomorrow and if he's likely to be drunk then you really should give me a hint."

"Drunk? Greg?"

"That's what I thought at first," Arne then explained his conversation with Martin.

She didn't look very convinced.

"I really don't know what's wrong with him, Arne. Despite what some people seem to think, the staff don't gossip about the patients and it isn't the cleaners who make the diagnosis."

"No, I suppose not, but I'm sure if you thought I'd be in danger you'd find a way to drop a hint."

"Maybe," Katie said. "But I don't have any reason to suppose Greg is a secret drinker. If the doctor is having tests done, that must be because they don't know what's wrong with him."

"I suppose."

The doorbell rang; it was Greg.

"I saw your light was on …"

"Come in, Greg. What's up?" Arne said.

"I've just checked the route for tomorrow and found out there are some road works. I think we should leave a bit earlier than we planned?"

"Good idea. Er, Greg, I was just wondering if you'd got results from that test you were having. What was it again?"

"Doctor called it a liver function test, but when I went in, all they did was take a blood sample. I haven't got the results yet."

"What are they looking for?"

"All kinds of things. I can't say the names of them, but

I've got a leaflet if you're interested?"

Arne wasn't really that interested, but it was his own fault for bringing up the subject.

"I'll put the kettle on," Katie said.

Greg came back with his leaflet and rambled on for quite a while about what could be wrong with his liver.

"I'm not sure I even know what the liver is supposed to do," Arne admitted as he drained his mug.

"I do, since I got this," Greg pointed to his slightly yellow face. "I've been reading up on it." He began to explain – in detail.

Arne was glad when Greg paused to drink some of his tea. His relief was short lived.

Drinking the tea gave him a second wind and he went on and on about yellow bile and the rest of him turning yellow too.

"Jaundice, isn't that what it's called?" Katie asked as she appeared from the kitchen to offer another brew.

She was probably just trying to help move the conversation along, but Greg took her comment as a sign of interest and gave Arne a complete run down on every possible cause of his problems and all potential outcomes. He was still going strong when Katie returned with more tea and a plate of biscuits.

His hosts were bored rigid, but talking about his illness seemed to have really cheered Greg up. He was quite chirpy when, after finishing his third mug of tea, he eventually said goodnight.

"Thanks for listening, Arne. Talking to you has helped me realise that the doctor is doing his best for me and that we'll soon know what's wrong. I owe you a drink; I'll buy you one tomorrow."

Arne cheered up himself, until he remembered Greg's idea of a nice drink was a warm can of Diet Coke.

"Thanks, mate," he muttered as he saw him out.

Arne felt he'd wasted hours of his life thanks to Martin jumping to conclusions and spreading rumours. He called after Greg, "By the way, Martin was asking about your health and seemed quite concerned. Can you explain it all to him? I know he'll be fascinated."

14. Juliet's Voice

Juliet Greenman coughed, earning herself another exaggerated sigh from her cousin Colin Dalgleish. He was almost as dismissive of her now as he had been when they were children. He'd had an excuse then; she'd been a quiet little thing two years his junior. These days she felt she deserved at least professional respect from him.

A colleague leant across Colin and slid the carafe of water to Juliet.

"Thanks," she croaked. The water soothed her burning throat a little, but soon she was coughing again. She supposed it was one way to attract Colin's attention. Usually he pretended not to notice her until he wanted coffee. Fetching it meant she often missed important decisions. Junior staff were emailed with the news but nobody thought to include Juliet, as she'd attended the meeting, so she was always the last to know.

She wondered if it was worth staying and annoying everyone with her cough, especially as she was overworked. Her hints she could do with an assistant had come to nothing. If she stopped attending the meetings Colin wouldn't care, he might not even notice until he became thirsty.

He was aware of her presence now, but it wasn't because of anything clever she had to say. Just her awful hacking cough. Her throat felt as though she'd eaten the shattered remains of the bowl that morning rather than her muesli. Whenever she so much as drew breath in preparation to speak, the coughing started again. Not waiting for Colin to say, "Coffee would be nice," she slipped out and switched on the kettle.

As Juliet mixed herself a Lemsip she brooded on her position at Dalgleish and Sons. People often assumed family connections got her and Colin where they were. It wasn't true. Although Colin occasionally encouraged people to think his name on the letterheads meant more than it did, he'd earned his role in the company. Juliet too was good at her job and worked hard. She certainly didn't owe it to Colin to struggle on whilst she was feeling ill so, as well as the coffee, she gave everyone the news she was going home. Her hoarse whisper got no reaction, so she grabbed a magic marker and scrawled a note over Colin's desk pad.

At home, the dishwasher door was open, exposing a full load of dirty crockery. On the kitchen table was her son's mug. Before she'd left for work, she'd asked him to put it in and switch on the machine. She knew what he'd say if she mentioned it.

"Sorry, Mum. I forgot."

Juliet performed the simple task herself before crawling into bed.

Both children and her husband came up at regular intervals that evening. They brought hot drinks and food. She tried to thank them, but her voice was gone.

Next morning Juliet dragged herself downstairs. Her husband and daughter had gone to work. Her son was there drinking his coffee.

"Feeling better?" he asked.

She tried to speak, but the effort hurt her throat without producing a sound. She got out a notepad intending to ask him to ring work, but realised no one would have arrived. Instead she wrote, 'Please put mug in dishwasher and switch on before you leave. Thanks. x' and went back to bed.

Juliet awoke an hour later to the sound of the dishwasher working. She emailed work to explain she felt no better. In reply she got sympathy, a copy of the minutes of the meeting and a message from Colin saying, 'If you feel up to it could you read these and let me know if you approve of the actions we've suggested?'

Wow! He had noticed her absence then. She read them and replied, giving her approval. As always, Colin's proposals were sound.

The doorbell rang. Juliet was tempted to ignore it, and when she opened the door, notepad at the ready, really wished she had.

Her neighbour held a child towards Juliet. "Hi. Could you just mind Timmy while I nip down the shops?"

She'd been caught like that before and ended up babysitting all day. Glad the notepad prevented the child being thrust into her arms, Juliet wrote, 'Can't take him. Bad cold. Infectious.'

"Don't worry. If it's something going round he's bound to catch it anyway."

'Can't take him. Too ill.'

"He wouldn't be any trouble at all."

Juliet wondered why, if he was so little trouble, his mother couldn't keep him. As she couldn't ask, she waved the note until the woman got the message and left with a not terribly gracious, "Hope you feel better soon."

Juliet was fine the following week, except when she tried to speak. No sound came, and if she persevered the coughing started again. She stopped trying.

Armed with her notepad she returned to work. Juliet discovered people couldn't talk over a note stuck under their nose, or not listen, so all her suggestions were at least considered.

The notes were valuable at home too. Her family didn't forget to put dirty laundry in the basket or empty the dustbin, because a note reminded them. Her husband didn't miss subtle hints about which programme she'd like to watch, or what she'd like to do at the weekend as notes made her wishes clear. He didn't always go along with them. She didn't expect, or even want, him to do exactly as she requested every single time, but she got her way about half the time. That was fair.

Friends didn't talk her into doing things she didn't want to, because writing her reply gave her thinking time. Normally her murmured, "I'm not sure," got swept aside with the other person's enthusiasm. On paper it was so much easier to write, 'Sorry, but I'd rather not'.

Her voice didn't return. Juliet decided she'd better get checked in case there was something more serious wrong than the lingering affects of her cold. Her puzzled doctor referred her to a specialist. The private medical care, provided by Dalgleish and Sons, ensured she didn't have to wait long.

"The tests are perfectly clear, Mrs Greenman and I can assure you there's nothing to worry about." The specialist said. "You have a rare form of chronic laryngitis. Your condition will probably begin to resolve itself in six months or so, but we can restore your voice much more quickly with medication and vocal therapy." He explained the procedure. "Any questions?"

'No', she wrote.

"OK good, we'll schedule you in then. Next Tuesday OK?"

She tapped the 'no' note.

He studied his diary. "I don't have another space for two weeks. Tuesday would be best."

'No'.

"All right. I'll put you down for the seventeenth."

She placed her note on his diary.

When he looked up she wrote another. 'I don't mind not speaking as long as there's nothing else wrong.'

"You're perfectly healthy otherwise. It's really not practical not to have a voice though."

As he listed all the inconveniences of being unable to speak, Juliet wrote, 'Thank you. Goodbye.' She practically skipped out the consulting room.

At work, via notes, she explained her voice wasn't likely to return quickly. She wrote, 'I think I will need an assistant to make calls for me.' She crossed through the first two words before passing it to Colin.

"Maybe we could advertise internally and see if any existing staff are interested?" he suggested.

'Good idea. Thank you,' she wrote. She knew the junior staff and quickly found someone suitable who was keen to accept a slight promotion. She had the girl transferred immediately.

Juliet was relieved to be able to stop making deals by

phone. She was always persuaded to sell more cheaply or buy more expensively than when she negotiated by letter or email. With her assistant making the calls and saying, "Sorry, Mrs Greenman won't authorise that," her deals were completed on much better terms.

Buoyed with her successes she asked her husband to make a dental appointment for her.

"Would you like me to come?" he asked.

Bless him, he understood her concerns about having all that treatment. Of course he did. She was due to start it whilst she had the cold. He'd cancelled for her and she'd explained to him, in writing, that she dreaded it.

'There's no need for you to come, but please explain about my voice.'

The dentist invited her to take a seat. Juliet didn't occupy the huge treatment chair, but sat on the one where she usually placed her handbag. She produced her prepared note asking what treatment was necessary to prevent pain and decay and which purely cosmetic.

"Mrs Greenman, I'm sure you'll find the whole course of treatment beneficial."

Momentarily it felt like she was lying back, light shining in her eyes and mouth full of instruments. Then Juliet pointed at her note, indicating she wanted an answer.

"Well… I suppose really it is more cosmetic than actually essential to preserve your teeth, but having a good smile is so important to a person's confidence."

Juliet had a good smile. Her husband said it was one of the things which first drew him to her. Her teeth hadn't changed, her smile only suffered from lack of use. It was buried under the pressure of her life and struggle to make herself heard.

She gave an experimental lift to the corners of her mouth. It felt all right. Quite good in fact.

She wrote another note. 'I've decided against the treatment. Will see you in six months for my check-up.'

Juliet returned to work. She stood outside and looked up at the huge sign saying 'Dalgleish and Sons.'

The Mr Dalgleish who'd started the company ordered it when his first son was born. The son had only one child, a daughter. He'd brought her in during school holidays and then permanently when she left school. She'd learned a great deal about the business by watching and listening to her father. In his shadow Juliet learned everything she needed to know, except how to speak for herself.

Now at last she'd found her voice. She strode inside and headed for Colin's office. She wrote him a note. 'I'm changing the company name.'

"I'm not sure you can do that." Colin sounded unhappy.

'Of course I can. I own it. I'm not a Dalgleish any more and I never was anyone's son.'

He nodded, looking even more miserable. "What do you propose? Greenman's?"

She gestured for him to move aside. Then typed onto his computer, 'Such a drastic change would mean more than just altering the stationery. We'd lose the reputation that's been built up since our Granddad started the firm. How about we call it Dalgleish and Family?'

"An excellent idea, cousin!"

She typed, 'Keep listening to me. I'll have more now I've found my voice.'

15. No Words

"Jade is a sweetie but …" My friend Ronnie said. "You can't talk to her, can you? What I mean is, it's not the same as …"

"As having a boyfriend?"

"Exactly."

She had a point. Jade, unlike her father and the men I've met since he left us, is a sweetie. OK, we don't have long, meaningful discussions, but she loves me even though juggling her care and working to support her mean sometimes I'm tired and grouchy. Jade wouldn't swap me for another mummy who's thinner, prettier, better. I wouldn't change her for anything, or anyone.

I've tried telling Ronnie all this before. Her response is always, "Not all men are the same, Lizzy."

"No? I suppose some only consider a kid as 'baggage' when it's not their own."

"You can't blame Jade for all your problems with men."

"I don't and don't you dare say I do!"

Ronnie just smiled. "I'll sign you up for the speed dating then. I'll babysit."

That suggestion had started the conversation. There seemed only one way to end it. "OK, but if it's another dead loss, you'll stop trying to fix me up?"

She's been trying to find my Mr Perfect since Jade's dad decided we weren't good enough for him. Some of the men she'd introduced me to seemed quite nice. A few got as far as meeting Jade. OK, so maybe I am a little over protective and a little too quick to assume any awkwardness around her is a problem that can't be overcome, but I won't have my darling daughter thought of in the same breath as baggage, handicap or disadvantage.

"If you give it a fair chance and nobody shows promise, then yes," Ronnie agreed.

On the day I had a really sore throat and rang Ronnie to croak, "I'm going to have to cancel."

"Great idea, Lizzy. You explain to Jade that she's not coming over here to play with her friends. Make sure you're really clear that having trouble speaking and making yourself understood means you have to give up on an evening out, or of giving yourself the chance of happiness, because that's a really important life lesson."

The rude name I yelled at her didn't help my sore throat. Neither did it shut her up.

"See, you can communicate perfectly well. Gargle with antiseptic and I'll see you about seven."

When I dropped Jade off, I didn't speak to Ronnie. I did try saying goodbye to Jade, but she'd already run off to join Ronnie's kids and the three of them were dancing away to imaginary music. No words were necessary for me to know she'd have a good time.

Ronnie said I should give the speed-daters a chance, so I wrote 'sorry, I can't speak' in my notebook and showed it to each in turn. Most talked about themselves. A few asked me questions, but grew impatient with my attempts to reply.

One man was different. Jim, first expressed sympathy, then asked, "Why not?"

"Sore throat," I wrote.

"Ah! I wondered if I was going to have an extra incentive for learning sign language."

I curled my fingers in a 'give me more' gesture.

"My friend's son is deaf, so I'm trying to learn."

He didn't say he had to do it, as indeed he didn't. He cared enough to try.

"What's his name?" I scrawled.

Jim touched his thumb, then laid his first finger across his palm, touched his thumb again, then put two fingers in his palm. "I just spelled out, ALAN," he said.

The next few minutes went by in a blur of written questions and answers. I hadn't finished reading them all when the buzzer sounded and Jim, reluctantly I thought, moved on.

At the end of the evening several men ticked the box saying they'd like to see me again. All but one were those who'd just talked about themselves and not learned a single thing about me. Jim was the exception. His was the only name I put a tick against.

When I got back to Ronnie's I read Jim's answers again. Nowhere did it say that one day he'd ask my daughter her name and that, after watching his lips, she'd spell out JADE. None of my questions asked if he'd consider my daughter as baggage, or whether he'd think her deafness a handicap or another incentive to learn sign language. Some things don't need words though, do they?

16. Special Interest Publication

Kitty stowed the magazine in her bag with a sigh of satisfaction. She was looking forward to the expressions on her fellow passengers' faces as the five-foot-nothing, mini-skirted, redhead opposite began to read *Tractor Enthusiasts Monthly*. She was so pleased she'd bought that rather than any of the other magazines she'd considered.

Although the article about the history of Massey Ferguson engines was well written, Kitty found her mind drifting to an evening a few days previously. Kitty had sighed: the on-line survey had made her feel inadequate. She was only completing it because doing so allowed her to enter a free draw. The prize was a year's subscription to a magazine of her choice.

One question asked which was her favourite brand of coffee. The choices included something organic and monsoon-washed for cafeterias or a secret blend of dark roasted ethically-sourced beans, coarse ground for filters. There wasn't a box for 'whichever half decent instant is on special offer' so she selected 'other'.

The question about cosmetics listed items she'd never heard of and which contained ingredients seemingly invented by someone addicted to anagrams. There was no box for the brand of lipstick she'd got free with her latest slushy paperback. Kitty answered 'other'. That's what she'd be buying next anyway. The free one was a lovely colour, but didn't seem to be on sale anywhere.

'Interests' was the next category. She thought, wrongly, that she'd be able to give an actual opinion there and justify her entry into the draw. Clicking 'cultural events' showed how different she was from the women the survey was aimed at. She liked to watch dramas on TV and read books. The survey wanted information on theatres and the Bronte sisters. Her latest slushy paperback that came with a free lipstick wasn't listed…

Kitty began to feel she wasn't listed. She completed the survey and tapped in her contact details, just in case she was a lucky winner. It could happen; she'd once won some very classy cheese in a competition she'd found on a packet of crackers. Of course, this survey wasn't interested in which type of classy cheese she ate. The only time she'd ticked anything except 'other' had been to answer the question about her favourite classical composer. Her paper gave away a Mozart cd last week, so she put his name down.

'Thank you for completing our survey', the website displayed. She was directed to a page advertising magazine subscriptions she could purchase and an assurance that, were she to win the competition after doing so, her money would be refunded.

Kitty had no trouble deciding which magazine she'd select if she won. It'd be the gardening one as she could give it to her mother-in-law. None of the others appealed. Kitty's family didn't follow a vegan diet so the cookery mag wouldn't get much use. She didn't crochet anything and doubted the 'beautifully detailed illustrations and step by step instructions' would encourage her to start. Never mind, she only had the chance to win one so wouldn't have to choose between antiques and homes abroad.

Although she wasn't interested in subscribing to those offered, buying a copy of a magazine that did interest her was a good idea. She had a long train journey for a work meeting. She'd learnt the hard way that reading an attention grabbing novel was an excellent way of missing her stop. A magazine would be better as she could check where she was after each article.

The newsagent's had a wider selection of magazines than she'd expected. She instantly dismissed the middle row; teenage music mags and gossip glossies. She wasn't a teenager and wasn't interested in the tiny details of Z-list celebrity lifestyles. She wasn't all that bothered by the major events in the lives of A-listers either. Her favourite weekly was there of course, but she'd already finished the current issue.

The bottom row was also dismissed. Her dad might like the fishing ones and mother-in-law would like the gardening ones, but Kitty wasn't interested. Something from the top shelf would either guarantee she got plenty of space on the train or have someone unsavoury breathing on her neck while trying to read over her shoulder.

Kitty had never looked along the top shelf before. Some of the magazines seemed very specialised. Curiously, she opened one that catered for those who were unusually fond of vinyl boots. The models seemed to share the readers' interest to such an extent they all wore the boots – and nothing else.

She replaced the mag and sighed; surely there was something to suit her? Kitty looked to see if there was one titled 'other'. There wasn't.

"Can I help you?" a lady asked.

"I will buy something, I promise. It's just that I'm not sure what."

"You're welcome to browse, dear, but if you'd like any help …?"

"I just want something to fill in time …"

"Nursing Times? Yes, we've got that."

"No, it's for reading on the train."

"All the train ones are here, under 'rail'."

The rail section was huge. It made Kitty hope she wouldn't have to wait long on any station platforms. She shook her head.

"Wait a tick; I'll get my hearing aid," the shopkeeper said.

When she returned, Kitty explained again why she wanted the magazine.

"Oh, I see! Sorry about that. Now you tell me about your interests and I'll find something suitable."

"I'm not sure that will help. I'm starting to feel no one has the same interests as me."

"We sell some very specialised magazines, I'm sure I can find something."

Noticing the booklet published by the local church and remembering the top shelf, Kitty agreed the shop did seem to cater for all tastes. She told the lady about her feelings of inadequacy while completing the survey. The lady looked thoughtful for a moment and then broke into a broad grin.

"There you go, dear; The very thing."

Kitty wasn't particularly interested in the article on anti-compaction tyres, or the report of the ploughing championship, but otherwise she was delighted with her purchase.

Not only would *Tractor Enthusiast's Monthly* give her fellow passengers something to think about, it included a survey for her to complete, four different competitions and came with a free bar of chocolate.

17. Just Two Little Words

Matthew stood at the alter gazing at his gorgeous, beloved Sonia. He only had to say, 'I do'. It wasn't much to ask, but his chest was so clogged with emotion he wasn't sure he'd be able to force those two little words into his throat.

Sonia looked up at him, showing just a hint of nerves and Matthew remembered the first time he'd seen her. She'd been in her 'room to grow' school uniform and gazed up at him from her huge blue eyes.

Her mum, Jean, had introduced them and said, "He's a new boy too and will look after you, just like I told you. Now have a good day, Sonia. I'll be waiting at the gate when you finish."

Jean was in the front pew now, wearing an enormous hat and waiting for him to speak. She'd not changed nearly as much as her daughter.

She, Sonia, had smiled that first day, revealing a gap at the front and a trusting nature. She'd looked so like a typical schoolgirl right down to beribboned pigtails and grazed knee she'd have been perfect for a television advert. Matthew had probably loved her right then, although he didn't realise that at the time.

Matthew had only joined the school in September, but by the time Sonia arrived at half term he'd settled in, made friends and knew his way around. He guessed it would be harder for the new girl who'd just moved to the area after her parents' divorce. He'd probably have been asked to help anyone new and wouldn't have minded, but maybe he did take a little more trouble over her. Maybe because his own parents had divorced he'd felt sympathy, but it wasn't just that. Anyone who saw her seemed to instantly like her; want to make her happy.

He'd helped Sonia make friends, even though that meant she soon had no need of him. She never abandoned anyone who'd been kind to her though and she always brightened his day with her smile and cheerful chatter.

Matthew watched as Sonia grew up to be a young woman as beautiful on the outside as she was on the inside. Everyone loved her, even the boys who knew she'd never date them and the girls who weren't as slim, whose hair wasn't as glossy and who didn't get invited to so many parties. Matthew would do anything reasonable to make her happy, even on occasions doing something unreasonable such as the time he'd hired a machine to provide the snow she wished to have falling on her birthday. Jean, Sonia's mum, told him he needn't bother but Matthew hadn't minded the expense or the hours of clearing up the tiny scraps of paper the following day. Her squeal of delight had made it all worthwhile.

They stayed close, Matthew and Sonia. By then he'd become part of the family and admitted his love for her. Sonia loved him too, in a way. She told him so, before answering the phone to speak to her latest boyfriend.

He listened to her worries over men, and offered what advice he could, even though none of them were anywhere near good enough for her. Didn't know her like he did, care for her like he did. Some of her choices almost broke his heart. There'd been the boy who wanted to take her back to Australia with him. He'd seemed the worst from Matthew's point of view until the one who appeared determined to drag her into his own personal hell of drink and drugs.

Sonia lost to him on another continent would have been hard to take, Sonia lost even to herself was an unbearable thought. Matthew had gone to the police. Had the man arrested, knowing Sonia would hate him for it. She did and that hurt, but not as much as attending her funeral would have done. He asked Jean to explain that, but it hadn't helped much.

They'd seen in the paper, many months later, the report of a couple, high on drugs who'd died in a house fire.

"Could have been me, couldn't it?" she whispered.

Matthew had nodded, tears in his eye. Not at the thought of losing her, but from the emotional response at knowing he'd regained her trust.

Then had come Gareth. In truth Gareth had always been around, ever since he'd been in Matthew's scout group. The boys had stayed in contact, even when Gareth went away to university. Then Gareth came back. He was attractive, charming and friendly, educated and employed, reliable and helpful. Matthew was tempted to try and keep his friends apart, but he could see that wouldn't be possible.

Sonia liked Gareth immediately, just as Matthew guessed she would. Over the next few months, Matthew swallowed his jealousy and plastered on a smile as he saw how happy Gareth made Sonia. Most importantly, Gareth loved Sonia. Really loved her. Sonia loved him. Jean loved him; Gareth was everything she could want in a son-in-law. Even Matthew had to admit he'd make a good husband for Sonia.

Matthew stood at the alter gazing at his gorgeous, beloved Sonia.

The minister asked, 'Who gives this woman to be married to this man?'

He only had to say, 'I do'.

Maybe to her it hadn't seemed much to ask, but for him they'd be the hardest two words he'd ever have to say. Matthew gazed at the girl whose friend he'd been since she was seven, whom he'd loved, it seemed, forever. Matthew swallowed hard and forced out the correct reply.

He was rewarded by her radiant smile and knew he'd done the right thing. She loved him too, as the step-brother he'd become when his dad married her mother. Loved him like a brother. It was time to accept Sonia would never be his and look elsewhere for love.

As Matthew made that decision he glanced over at the bridesmaids. Gareth's younger sister gave him a cheeky grin. Maybe the reception wasn't going to be quite as heartbreaking as he'd feared.

18. The Big Picture

People had always told Sienna she was a dreamer. When Mum asked her three times to do the dishes she knew Sienna wasn't being stubborn; she'd just not heard. Instead she'd been thinking about the wonderful future which would soon be hers. Friends admired her ambition and were jealous of her ability to be somewhere far more exciting even when sitting next to them in maths.

Teachers were less impressed, saying she was too much of a dreamer to ever achieve anything. Didn't they realise her talent of thinking herself somewhere, or even someone, else was what made her such a brilliant actress.

Sienna had been superb as Snow White in the school play. She'd thought herself into the part. When Rachel, playing the wicked stepmother, offered her an apple, Sienna knew it was poisoned. Rachel had been jealous of her getting the starring role and tampered with it. Sienna, unable to let down her audience, had eaten it and fallen into her long sleep tragically and beautifully. Everyone said so.

A few also commented she'd occasionally forgotten her lines. Some people had to focus on the little details because, unlike Sienna, they couldn't see the bigger picture. That was all years ago. Now she was about to prove her doubters wrong.

She still had the bigger picture clear in her mind. No one was likely to forget they were about to be presented with their first BAFTA were they? She hadn't neglected the little details though. Her acceptance speech was written and she'd practised giving it dozens of times. She couldn't be sure how emotional she'd feel, so kept it short. Everyone would understand if her voice wobbled and a single glistening tear slid down her face, but she didn't want to be still up on stage blubbing as mascara dripped off her nose because she hadn't reached the part where she thanked everyone who'd believed in her.

Her outfit was sorted too. The shoes, dress, jewellery. It was perfect, all of it. It fitted well; no chance of rips or slips to result in an embarrassing wardrobe malfunction. She'd practised sitting in her outfit, standing, walking and climbing a few steps. Sienna had even tried curtseying and then laughed. That was getting a little ahead of herself.

Simple and understated, that's how her look might be described. Sienna wasn't a big Hollywood name with fashion houses clamouring to dress her. Not yet. She'd bought everything in the High Street. The women's magazines would love that. They'd do features explaining how readers could copy every detail.

Publicity like that was important. Sienna's status as a new sensation and overnight success wouldn't last long. She'd have to make the most of it. No doubt the newspapers and television would want to interview her. She'd anticipated a few questions and rehearsed answers. No detail was too important to escape her attention. Sienna had even practised sipping champagne without getting lipstick on her glass.

Everyone was going to be so impressed. No one would ever again say she was too much of a dreamer to achieve anything. They couldn't could they? Not after they'd seen her on the red carpet, her leading man looking adoringly at her and the paparazzi begging for a smile.

Sienna's thoughts were interrupted by a tap on her bedroom door.

Mum looked in. "I've come to see if you'd like help learning your lines? I know you said you've got it all under control, but your very first audition is bound to be a bit nerve wracking, so a last minute run through wouldn't hurt."

"Last minute?" Sienna said. "There's hours left yet." She ripped open the envelope she'd been sent three weeks previously, and started reading the script.

19. Playing Politics

It all started when I was down the library, trying to find an Agatha Christie I hadn't read. It's a tiny little branch which only opens two afternoons a week and very rarely gets new stock, so I wasn't hopeful.

With difficulty and a few painful twinges I'd managed to crouch down and inspect the lowest shelf. It hadn't been a rewarding experience and I still had to get up.

"Hello, Mary. Need a hand?" a voice I recognised asked.

"Thank you," I said as Judy hauled me up. Although grateful for her assistance I was wary. I've known Judy since our daughters were at school together twenty-odd years ago and she's always been a bit alarming. Many's the time I'd bought cakes, messed up the icing a little and stuck them in tupperware containers because she'd demanded I bake to help the P.T.A. raise funds.

There was barely a, "Nice to see you. How are you?" exchanged before she launched her latest attack. She wanted me to help her with some protest she was trying to get up about having the bins emptied more often.

"Sorry, I don't see how I can help. I'm not fit enough for marching or chaining myself to railings." She knew ill health had forced me to give up my job, but knowing Judy she'd just think that meant I had more time to help her campaign.

"Everyone can help in some way. I thought you could

talk to James Stall. He lives near you, doesn't he?"

"Yes," I admitted. Had to really as he's right next door. "I don't talk to him much though."

"Well it's time to start, Mary," she said and instructed me in what to say.

Mercifully her phone rang soon afterwards. She went outside to answer it. I was able to escape while she was still in conversation.

As I walked slowly home I thought about what Judy had said. In theory I agreed with her. Waiting two weeks between rubbish collections was inconvenient as manoeuvring a full bin was very difficult for me. Cleaning it was a problem too. As I'd told her though, I didn't feel there was much I could do. James is a local councillor, so I could see why she wanted me to speak to him, but I was reluctant to try.

He's a bit on the nosy side, I've always thought. He really only asked the same kind of questions as anyone else, but it was the way he asked; as though he actually wanted to know. That might seem a strange complaint, but think about it. When you meet anyone, other than your very nearest and dearest, although you might say 'how are you?' you don't really want to know. It's politeness to ask. And it's polite to give a reply anywhere in the range of 'fine thanks' to 'not so bad'. If your knee is giving you gyp or you've got an unexplained rash, you tell the doctor, not a chance met acquaintance. If you do happen to hear about someone's hot flush or ingrown toenail, the thing to do is utter a vague hope it'll be better soon and change the subject.

I'm maybe giving the wrong impression of James. He didn't ask impertinent medical questions. He didn't ask any impertinent questions at all. Somehow though he had a way of getting you to tell him things. Maybe I noticed it more because of my condition. Don't worry I'm not going to go into details! I try to stay as active as I can and take several short walks a day. If James doesn't catch me on the way out, he does on my way back. Oh well, I thought, next time he does I'll mention the bins.

Just for once James wasn't waiting to accost me. Even better, the postman had left a letter telling me I'd got the job I'd applied for. Perfect for me it was. Working from home, typing notes and proofreading reports for one of the political parties. I won't say which, I don't think that'd be fair. In any case, I had to sign all kinds of confidentiality paperwork so I could get into trouble. My life isn't a secret though – not any more!

I started straight away and although that meant I didn't talk to James for a few days I learned he was an influential party member as well as a councillor. I discovered James was making reports on me. Not just me, but a lot of it was. 'What the man on the street thinks' that's what he claimed to be reporting. What the woman next door says is what he actually wrote about. Oh he kept names and all that out of it, but I recognised my own words all right. It seemed the pedestrian crossing near the library would be adjusted to allow people longer to get over the road before the lights changed, more or less on my say so. My words had power!

I'd been a dead loss on the homemade cake deal, but I was determined to do Judy proud over the bins. Three times the following week I had fish for tea. Not the stuff in batter, but whole ones bought in town with the heads still on. You can imagine how they stank by the time I asked James if he could help with my bin as I wasn't strong enough when it was really full. I added concerns about hygiene and attracting rats and what were we paying rates for if it wasn't to have the bins emptied?

My efforts worked out very well. Not only did we go back to weekly bin collections, I got lots of work typing up and checking information leaflets telling people what the council tax is used for.

Must dash, I can see James coming home and I want to remind him the library is short on Agatha Christie's books.

20. King Of The Castle

"I'm the king of the castle, get down you dirty rascal."

Flora ran to the barred window and looked down from the tower. It was all right; the small boy chanting the words was laughing and pointing at a bigger version of himself. The older boy, presumably his brother, laughed back while waving a plastic sword.

She should be used to that particular phrase, but six years of hearing it used in fun whilst working at Solent Castle hadn't been enough to erase painful childhood memories. Even now she was king of the castle and had the power to knock him down, Flora remembered the humiliation inflicted by Bryan Murray.

Whenever Flora had dared scramble over the climbing frame, Bryan rushed up the other side, screeching those terrible words.

"I'm the king of the castle, get down you dirty rascal."

Then he'd pushed her. Soft rubber under the play equipment meant Flora was never seriously injured, but the fall always hurt her pride.

If Flora was foolish enough to go near the big scary slide, Bryan would push and prod until her only route of escape was up the metal ladder. She'd tremble at the top as Bryan and his friends surrounded the slide. They called out, "Get down you dirty rascal," over and over until she hurtled down the slippery surface, letting out a yell loud enough to be heard by the whole playground.

When it was Flora's turn to stand at the front of the class and read poetry or say her three times table, Bryan would put a paper crown on his head. The words 'get down, get down' rang in her mind until she struggled to read words on the page or remember sums. She wasn't stupid, just shy. She knew that now, but at the time it seemed the confident Bryan really was king, of the class at least.

"He sounds like a bully to me, you keep away from him," had been Aunt Betty's advice.

Flora tried to do as her guardian suggested, but it wasn't easy. Bryan caught the same bus and had the desk in front of hers. She always used the awkward sideways seat at the front of the bus and got into classes early so she didn't have to pass Bryan.

"You'll have to practise harder," Aunt Betty said when Flora's school report showed she wasn't progressing so well with her lessons as she had the previous year.

The previous year, Mummy and Daddy weren't in heaven and she'd not been at the same school as Bryan Murray. Flora was confident and popular until a car crash had taken all that away from her. Flora had moved in with Aunt Betty. Bryan Murray's family lived in the same street and the bullying had started the first day she caught the bus to school and unknowingly sat in Bryan's favourite seat. Maybe it wouldn't have been so bad if she hadn't managed to get her new school sweatshirt splattered with mud at break time. In trying to wipe it off, she'd transferred some dirt to her face, and in an effort to hide the mess she'd folded the top and sat on it.

Bryan's chant of "Get down you dirty rascal," had sort of been appropriate then. If she'd given up the seat, or answered back, or wiped her face clean maybe that would have been the end of it, but she just sat there as though frozen until the teacher asked her what was wrong. Flora had repeated Bryan's words, much to the amusement of the whole class. Bryan had repeated the taunt at every opportunity for the rest of the term.

There wasn't anything much Aunt Betty could do about that, but she had taught Flora her times tables as well as lots of other things.

When they went to senior school, it was easier for Flora to avoid Bryan. He cycled to school and history was the only lesson they shared. Aunt Betty insisted Flora always did her homework and studied hard. Flora took extra trouble with history; she wouldn't let Bryan humiliate her.

"You're doing well with your lessons now, love," Aunt Betty said.

"That's because I've got no friends to go out with and just stay at home studying."

"Why don't you try for a Saturday job then? You'd get to meet some new people that way."

Flora began helping out in the gift shop at Solent Castle which did wonders for both her confidence and finances.

At university, Flora didn't see Bryan at all. He chose to study in a different part of the country. She heard a few reports of him from time to time; just enough to know they were both reading history and that he got a degree almost as good as hers. After her education, Flora was immediately accepted as assistant curator at Solent Castle. She knew she was lucky to get such a good job straight away. No doubt it helped that she'd worked there every weekend throughout her schooldays and every holiday since. Her hard work and enthusiasm ensured that when her boss retired, she was invited to take over from him. The young age at which she became curator made her something of a celebrity in her chosen field.

Flora was now about to move on to an even more prestigious position within the trust she worked for. Her assistant, Graeme, was to take over from her. Flora had the task of selecting a new assistant curator from the three who'd been shortlisted by the castle's trustees.

It appeared Bryan hadn't been so lucky with his career. He'd had a series of short term posts. Flora wondered why he'd moved on so many times. Was he still as unpleasant as he'd been as a boy, or were the rumours about him caring for his sick mother true? Whatever the reason, he was one of the people to be interviewed later that day. She'd gasped when she'd seen his name.

"You know him?" Graeme had asked.

"That's right."

"Good or bad?"

By answering that question, Flora could easily have ensured the only way Bryan ever saw Solent Castle was as a paying visitor. She could, but she wasn't sure she should. Bryan had probably changed a lot. He had been polite to her the few times they'd bumped into each other since they'd finished school and when she'd been featured in History Monthly, he'd cut out the article, drawn a crown on her photograph and sent it with a note saying 'you're Queen of the castle now - Congratulations.' Maybe competing against him at school had pushed her towards a successful career? No; Bryan didn't deserve any credit. Aunt Betty's encouragement and her own efforts were responsible for Flora's good fortune.

"I haven't seen him for a long time," was all Flora said.

She'd looked through the three candidates' files. All were equally well qualified. The only difference between them would be how they performed at interview. By choosing her questions carefully and making her feelings clear, Flora could easily influence the outcome. She wouldn't do that. Graeme would be the one to work closely with whoever was selected, she'd let him make the decision.

Flora was king of her castle now, but she never had been a dirty rascal and wouldn't let Bryan Murray turn her into one.

21. Fading Bruises

I'd been worried about Lisa for some time before I actually saw the bruises. Mostly it was just little things. The sunny week when she wore long sleeved tops to work instead of her usual pretty T-shirts is probably what first got me wondering. Occasionally wearing a thick layer of foundation over a face which was generally free of make-up was another indication. When I saw things like that I found myself twisting my wedding ring round in agitation, wondering what to do.

Sometimes Lisa declined invitations to socialise because she had to tend to Rhys. Almost every week someone in the office would suggest meeting up for a drink, meal, trip to the cinema or even to listen to a local band. Nobody went to everything; I was hardly ever able to go myself. It wouldn't have been surprising if Lisa just said it wasn't her kind of thing, or that she was busy. It wasn't that she said no, but the way she said it. Kind of wistful.

There was her knee too. That was clearly painful and the swelling was visible through her skinny jeans.

Now and again other colleagues noticed there was something wrong. They'd ask, "How did you do that?" or "What's up with your leg?"

Lisa always brushed it off with a laugh, as though it was nothing. "I fell," for her bruised face. "Thought the gateway was bigger," for her damaged knee. "Would you believe I walked into a tree?" to explain the black eye.

Usually there'd be some teasing about her clumsiness or bad luck. Generally though the excuses were accepted and her injuries forgotten by the others. I suppose she tried to forget them herself.

I didn't believe her. I was sure even then that Rhys had done those things to her and I was desperate to help. Maybe it's because that was my impulse the first time I saw her. She'd come for an interview and I happened to be the one who went down to meet her. Poor girl was in a state. An unexpected shower had drenched her, leaving her blouse almost transparent. She'd only realised after using the intercom to announce she'd arrived. As she stepped back she'd caught sight of her reflection.

By the time I got there she was hurrying away.

"Miss Bradshaw!" I called, rushing after her.

"I'm sorry to mess you about, but I can't go to an interview like this," she said.

Glancing at the bright scarlet, lacy bra and barely more muted rose tattoo I had to agree. "Not really, but is walking down the High Street a better option? Come on, we'll sort this out."

I took her into the ladies loo. She tried drying off under the hand drier, but I could see it would take ages and leave her red faced and sweaty.

"You'd better take it off," I said.

We switched blouses. The cold material of hers clung to my skin unpleasantly, but her smile of relieved gratitude made up for that. Once I had my cardigan done up no one could tell what we'd done. I walked Lisa through the main office, carrying out a few hasty introductions before escorting her to the interview.

"As Miss Bradshaw was early, I've given her a quick tour," I said, just in case she was a little late by then.

On my way out I heard Lisa saying it seemed a very friendly place to work. Miss Jenkins, our boss, is very keen on team spirit and a happy work environment and all that, so I wasn't surprised Lisa got the job.

I was surprised by the lovely bouquet she bought me when she got her first month's pay. There was absolutely no need; she'd already thanked me profusely and I'd done almost nothing. Even so, I accepted them with pleasure. Knowing they were there on my desk made coming into work even more of a joy for the next week or so.

When I discovered Lisa had been born just two years after I got married, the almost motherly affection I felt for her deepened. If I'd had a child, he or she would be around the same age. Justin didn't want children. I've come to realise I was right to go along with his wishes, but sometimes I'll see a mother and daughter laughing together, or a son hugging his mum and have to hide my tears.

Yesterday, Lisa was carrying in a tray of teas and coffees when someone dropped their pen. She saw them push back their chair in time to sidestep out of the way, but knocked up against the photocopier. I saw the pain on her face and knew something was badly wrong. A cracked rib was my guess, but there were other possibilities.

I have tried, gently, to get her to confide in me. It was a long shot. It's a difficult thing to talk about because if you do, then it's no longer your guilty little secret. It's a real thing. You might have to take action and after so long that's a frightening thought. Somehow it seems safer to stick with what you know. Sometimes he's kind, you have a nice house and you know now that bruises fade, pain is temporary. Besides, where would you go? Who could you turn to? You have no one now except for him. Everyone else had to be kept at a distance so they couldn't see the truth and make you see it too.

It was different for Lisa though. She was young and bright and still had hope. She reminded me of myself twenty years ago. Back when I thought Justin's anger was something I could learn not to provoke. That him being sorry afterwards meant there wouldn't be a next time, or at least that it wouldn't be so bad.

"I know we don't have much in common," I said. "But I'd like to think we're friends," I said to her just last week.

"Of course, Anne. Is there something you wanted to talk about?"

"Me? Oh no, but if you ever do, well, I'd listen and I wouldn't judge and I'd help if I could."

"Thanks, Anne. Same here. I hope you know that."

She spoke gently, with concern. That's another trick used by people like us. If someone asks too many questions, seems to see below our public face, we turn it around. Ask about their lives. It almost always works.

It was just chance that I saw Lisa's bruises this morning. Since Justin was made redundant I've left home each morning as early as I can. Usually I walk slowly, but it was raining so I hurried and arrived early.

"Anne! You're in early!"

Lisa had got soaked by a motorist driving through a puddle, she told me. That's why she was trying to dry her T-shirt under the hand drier in the ladies.

"I promise I don't strip down to my bra every time I come into the office," she said.

Although I too recalled our first meeting, it wasn't her underwear, or the new tattoo, which held my attention. There were angry red toecap sized marks all down her left side and across her ribs. Marks that I knew from painful experience would become purple by the following day, would gradually merge into green the week after and then fade to yellow before disappearing. There might then be weeks, months if you were careful, before you made a mistake, said the wrong thing and they were replaced.

She saw me stare, realised why and said, "I fell."

Healthy young girls don't fall as often as Lisa claims to do. Middle aged woman don't fall as often as I've attributed injuries to that cause. Of course it happens sometimes, but slipping over doesn't cause bruises like that. I know what does.

"Lisa, did Rhys do this to you?"

"No. I fell, like I said. Really I did."

I'd been too direct, I saw that immediately. She'd answered by reflex, just as I had so many times before. I changed tack a little, spoke more softly. "He was there though?"

"Well yes, but it wasn't his fault."

"And when you hurt your knee and got that bruise around your eye?"

"I'm lazy and impatient sometimes. I bring it all on myself."

It was like listening to an echo of my own inner voice. I'd learned not to care much what happened to stupid, clumsy Anne, but I did care something about Lisa.

"It isn't your fault," I told her.

"Anne, you don't understand."

So I did the only thing I could and for the second time removed my blouse in front of her. I let her see the green tinged bruises mottling my back. They've been there weeks, but her gasp proved they were still visible.

"I was clumsy. I spilled his tea."

"Oh, Anne." She reached out a hand, but I wasn't finished.

I undid the floral print silk scarf from around my neck to reveal the pressure marks from his hands.

"I said I'd like to go with the rest of you to the Italian restaurant on Saturday. Stupid of course to rub it in that I'm the one who still has a job. Selfish to want to go out and have fun whilst Justin has to stay in with his whisky bottle. He was right to remind me. If I'd gone, he'd have got jealous and suspicious and angry by the time I got home and then …" I hitched up my skirt to show her the faded scars on my thigh.

"Anne, that's awful."

"Yes it is." I paused, wondering why I could say that to her and not to myself. "What he did was awful, but even worse is that I've let him do it again and again. I shouldn't have. Don't make my mistake. You tell yourself it was something you did, that he didn't mean it, that he'll stop… By the time you realise it's not your fault and he'll get worse not better, it's too late. There's no one who'll believe you. No one who cares. No one who can help."

"I believe you."

I nodded. Of course she did.

"I care." The tears in her eyes showed the truth of that.

"And I want to help," she said.

"You can't."

"I can if you let me. I'll come with you to the police or a solicitor if that's what you want." She produced a handful of leaflets and sheets of things downloaded from the internet. Advice on legal matters, shelter, people to talk to.

I was horrified. "Can you imagine what he'd do once he found out?"

I left him once. Got right away, but Justin doesn't allow me to carry more than ten pounds in cash as I'm careless and likely to lose it, so I used our joint bank card for the train fare and hotel room. He came and took me home.

He was gentle with me, saying he forgave me for the trouble and worry I'd brought him. He realised he'd frightened me and understood why I'd wanted a few days away.

Patiently he explained that he never wanted to hurt me but that sometimes my behaviour drove him to it. He forgave me that too. So kind was he that I knew he'd forgive me the next time I was clumsy, forgetful or failed to read his mind. That he'd forgive every mistake of mine that forced him to use his fists in the years ahead.

"He can't do anything to you if you're not there," Lisa said. "Leave him, Anne. You can stay with me until you get sorted and ..."

That was impossible, of course. I couldn't leave and risk everyone knowing what had happened. They'd despise me, think I deserved it. I've seen the look in the hospital as I've invented reasons for my injuries and assured the nurses my husband was waiting at home to look after me. It didn't show on the nurses' faces, but was clearly visible when I caught sight of my own reflection.

And concerns over Justin and myself were only half the problem. "Stay with you? And Rhys?"

"Rhys will be in his stable. He's a horse, Anne. Like I said, sometimes I fall. It's because I'm impatient and tried going over jumps before I'd had enough lessons, or once hadn't bothered to tighten the girth holding the saddle on. I smashed my knee because, instead of opening a gate properly, I tried to get him to squeeze through and it swung back on me."

My face must have made that stupefied expression it forms when Justin screams at me for a mistake I'd not realised I'd made, or accuses me of doing something he must know I wouldn't have dared even think of. Lisa didn't slap me, or shake me as I slowly sank down onto the floor. The shock of realising my secret was no longer hidden left me unable to stand.

Lisa sat down next to me and held my hand. "I got some teasing when I bought Rhys. A few friends thought I'd turned snobby, so I kept quiet about him. When Miss Jenkins asked about my bruises, I saw the possibility of getting you to tell the truth about yours."

"You lied to me?"

"No… but I did mislead you. I'm sorry, Anne but I had to do something. I've been worried for a long time. The first day we met, you had bruises. I'm so used to having them myself I hardly noticed. It took me too long to realise that the same was true of you."

It was true. I couldn't remember where, or why, I'd been hit on that occasion.

"Your injuries have been getting worse and you're hurt more often. We knew we had to do something to get you to admit what was happening before we could help you."

"We?" I looked around to see Miss Jenkins in the doorway.

"Anne, we know what's been happening and that it's not your fault," Miss Jenkins said. "We care and we want to help."

"Will you let us?" Lisa asked.

My confusion must have been obvious.

Miss Jenkins told us to get dressed, sent Lisa in to the main office and took me to hers. She gave me a cup of tea and left me with the leaflets to think.

Justin had been my husband for a long time. I'd loved him once and I knew that in his way he cared about me. Cared about me more than I did about myself. His need to be the only person of importance in my life had left me without family to turn to and no way to reach them if I had. We had the house together and so many shared memories, some very happy ones. We had our health and weren't yet old. There was a long future stretching ahead of us.

An hour or so later I'd almost made up my mind and went in search of Lisa.

"It's your decision," she said. "I'm your friend, remember. I'll do whatever you'll let me to help."

Not long after that, Miss Jenkins drove me home. Lisa came too.

"Would you like me to come in with you?" she asked.

"Yes, please, but not yet."

We waited until Justin left for his usual lunchtime trip

to the pub, then packed up my clothes and toiletries. I didn't need or want anything else.

I left a note, saying I would be staying with a friend for a few days. He wouldn't know where to look. Like me, he hadn't realised I had friends. People who care in a way which doesn't split lips or leave bruises. People who are helping me.

Justin isn't so lucky. He doesn't have any friends. But you know what, for the first time in years, I'm not worried about what he's going to do.

22. Love By The Book

Samantha studied the huge new sculpture outside the library. The two figures looked a bit like her and her mate Lou gossiping. Or maybe Lou trying, again, to set her up with her friend from amateur dramatics.

Samantha knew what she'd be saying. "I like doing the posters, Lou, but that's because it gets my artwork seen across town. It's not because I want to be fixed up."

Lou would roll her eyes and claim to have no idea what Samantha was talking about – then add that the man she had in mind was really sweet.

Today Samantha was alone. The library hadn't seemed the sort of place a cool, up-and-coming artist would go, so she'd intended to make the visit short. The sculpture outside and the art inside reassured her. After selecting the books she needed, she studied her surroundings. Maybe her own paintings would hang there one day?

Not every work of art in the library was hanging from the walls. One was walking towards her. At first glance Samantha saw he was composed of neat, rich brown hair, long limbs, broad shoulders and firm stomach, washed over with a healthy outdoors-liking tan and clothing which was both well cut and well ironed. Her second glance met his and she gazed into large hazel eyes. His lopsided grin revealed pretty good teeth and Samantha felt her lips curve to mirror his smile.

There was plenty to smile about. His strong arms

looked capable of a decent hug and led to clean, tidy, but not manicured hands clutching an armful of books. The two Samantha could identify were by Ed McBain. Good, if he had time to read them he was probably single and, as she liked McBain too, they had similar tastes. Maybe they could travel to New York and visit Steve Carella's patch.

Samantha's fantasy was spoilt by the realisation Mr Artwork On Legs was studying her own book choices. They were on goat keeping, domestic egg production and grassland management; research for a painting. Together with hair stiff from turpentine and paint-spattered overalls she looked more scary hippy than chic artist. Never mind, she'd return when she hadn't suddenly had the idea to set her painting of toy cows in a real farmyard. Anyone who borrowed books by the armful was probably a regular visitor to the library.

Hoping Mr Artwork's visit was part of a routine, Samantha returned to the library a week later; after she'd blow-dried her hair and changed into a pretty top and figure flattering jeans. She arrived just in time to see him walk into the room signed 'Quitting smoking? We can help'. That was excellent – both that he was giving up the unhealthy habit and that she now knew he'd be coming back each week. That meant there was no rush to attempt to form a relationship. On the other hand, why wait longer than necessary? Samantha went for a coffee and returned an hour later.

Although it was the readers, or rather one reader in particular, she sought Samantha ensured her attention appeared to be on the reading matter. Soon she'd found a book to help her convince Lou that taking the first ever female lead in The Singing Detective would be a mistake.

"Hi."

Samantha looked up into the amused face of her attractive quarry.

"Found what you were looking for?" Mr Walking Artwork asked.

Samantha felt her face glow, though she wasn't sure if it was because he'd realised she'd been looking for him or because the book she was holding was on skin diseases.

"Yes, thanks. Uh, gotta go," she mumbled before he could wonder if her blush was caused by anything contagious.

Samantha tried again the following week. She managed to exchange a few words with him about a book he was holding. Not an Ed McBain, but judging from the cover it was somewhat similar.

"Do take it if you're interested," he very kindly offered.

Just when she thought she was getting somewhere, he seemed distracted by the pretty blonde waiting impatiently at the counter.

On three separate visits, after spotting her good looking Ed McBain fan, Samantha raced outside then strolled up and down, so she'd just happen to be passing when he came out. He never appeared.

Lou wasn't sympathetic. "You can't just get a man from the library, Sam. You have to get to know people."

"Like you do at Am Dram?"

"Yes. I know quite a bit about the friend I was telling you about."

"Hmm. Well, actually you can tell a lot about a bloke by what he reads. I'd be warned in advance if he had an obsessive interest in restoring aqueducts or the history of cricket in the Middle East."

"There are books on those things?"

"Yep. I think he picked them up by mistake though as I saw him putting them back."

Samantha didn't mention that Mr Artwork's selections were so random she didn't feel she was getting to know him at all.

On her next attempt, Samantha took as much care over her book selection as on choosing her dress and removing every scrap of paint from her fingers. She picked a funny novel, to show her sense of humour, and one on cake making as she really was interested in that and Granny always said the way to a man's heart was through his stomach. She briefly considered choosing one on massage, but could imagine what Granny or even Lou might say about that – and they'd be right.

It didn't take Samantha long to spot her real reason for being there. He looked as good as ever, but carried books on advanced origami, care of tarantulas and creative ways with anchovies. She backed away slowly to the safety of large print fiction, then made a run for it.

This time, Lou was more encouraging. A lot more. "Give him another chance. He sounds nice and you wouldn't want him to judge you on some of your book choices."

"Why not?"

Lou held up *Easy Bakes and Tempting Treats* and *Practical Poisons*. "He might not want to come to tea. In fact, I'm not sure I want to finish this piece of coffee and walnut. Doesn't coffee mask the bitter taste of poison?"

"I don't know. I just wanted a clear image of poison for

the *Hamlet* poster."

"Taking the books back tomorrow morning, are you?"

"Probably."

"I would. Just before lunch would be a good time."

Samantha was suspicious over her friend's sudden change of mind about the suitability of the library as a place to meet someone, but then remembered she'd had an Am Dram rehearsal the previous night. Presumably the man Lou had been trying to persuade her to meet was no longer available and she'd given up trying to fix Samantha up.

When Samantha arrived at the library, Mr Artwork was outside, leant against the sculpture, reading *Hamlet*. She waited until he looked up to explain her interest in poisons.

"Oh, you're Samantha the artist! That explains your eclectic taste in books."

"Do you have a similarly good excuse for yours?"

"For most of them. I'm a librarian so was returning them to the shelves."

"Ooops! Yes, good excuse."

He held up *Hamlet*. "Not sure you'll think the same about this. I'm preparing for my role in the play."

"Oh!"

"I'm meeting our mutual friend Lou for lunch, care to join us?"

23. Over My Dead Body

When Steve told his mum he was getting married she'd sniffed and said, "I thought as much."

Janine knew her prospective mother-in-law fairly well by then and so tried not to be offended by what from anyone else would have seemed a distinct lack of enthusiasm. She'd not yet heard her saying it, but Steve had told her that if Mum disapproved she made it clear by folding her arms and quietly stating 'over my dead body'.

Although Mum had clearly thought they were making rather a fuss compared with the simple church service followed by tea in the village hall which she'd had, those dread words hadn't been heard once during the wedding preparations.

"It's up to you I suppose," she said each time Steve or Janine had shared any plans with her.

Janine was the only child of fairly wealthy parents and her father had put aside a generous sum for her big day. Steve was also an only child, but his mum had struggled to feed and clothe him properly after her husband's death when he was just four. They could see why Mum found it difficult to understand the care with which they selected napkins in the exact shade of blue as the bridesmaids' dresses.

Janine had feared the worst when she tentatively suggested Mum wear a fascinator. She had folded her arms. She'd looked determined. She'd spoken quietly. "If you want me to put something on my head it will be a proper hat, thank you very much."

When Janine hugged her she'd muttered, "Oh, get away with you!"

It wasn't until Steve and Janine's daughter was born that Mum strongly disagreed with any of their decisions. Janine intended to go back to work which meant arranging child care for the baby. They'd been having lunch when the subject was raised.

Mum dropped her cutlery onto her plate with a clatter. She pushed back her chair, folded her arms and almost whispered, "Over my dead body."

"But, Mum, Janine has a job she's worked hard to qualify for, which she loves and which helps people. Besides …"

"That's as maybe, but if you think you're going to hand my granddaughter over to a stranger you've got another think coming. I'll look after her and the money you save can be put aside for her wedding like your dad did for you, Janine."

"Really? That's brilliant."

"Thank you, that would be much better," Steve added.

"Oh get away with you, the pair of you."

She'd been as good as her word and cared for Jemima and later Joshua very well. She had no truck with ready meals or plonking them in front of the TV for hours. They weren't quite spoiled, but her parents doubted their requests to play in the park, have an extra slice of cake or be read another story were ever met with a crossed arm refusal. That had come later.

Jemima had planned to have a tattoo. No one was quite

sure how Mum found out when the girl's brother and parents didn't have a clue, but she stepped in front of the girl as she was about to go into the parlour.

"You go in there over my dead body."

"But, Gran, it's MY body I want to get inked."

"You're my flesh and blood and I'm not having you… Oh, I suppose it is your body and your choice, but think it over a bit more will you? Come on, buy your old Gran a cup of tea and tell me why you want to do this."

Over tea Jemima had spoken enthusiastically about the design she wanted and how it expressed her personality and individuality, but somehow she never actually got it marked onto her skin.

When Joshua had dropped out of college she'd sent him back and said he'd leave again over her dead body. He'd completed his studies and eventually qualified as an accountant. Every year on the anniversary of the day he'd returned to education he sent his grandmother a gift. These had become increasingly more generous as his career advanced. She often told him not to waste his money, but he was good at choosing things she enjoyed and Mum was always persuaded to accept.

Recently he'd been made a partner and offered to send his gran on a cruise. Everyone expected a refusal but after reassuring herself he really could afford the ticket, she'd asked if it would be possible to take a round Britain trip.

"This country's good enough for me. There's plenty of it I haven't seen yet and after watching that Coast programme it seems like doing so from the sea is a good idea. Besides, I can't deny I like the idea of there being constant entertainment and activities laid on and having lots of people to talk to."

That's when it hit them she was lonely. Her grandchildren kept in touch with letters and phone calls, but she didn't see them very often. Steve and Janine often shared Sunday lunch with her and sometimes took her to the cinema or even a whole day out but that still left her alone through the working week.

"What can we do?" Janine asked her husband. "She doesn't need sheltered housing or someone coming in to look after her or anything like that."

"No and you can imagine what she'd say if we suggested it before it was absolutely necessary?"

"I can, yes. And she'd be the same about one of us retiring early to spend more time with her. She's never really had any hobbies or anything which involve mixing with people, has she?"

"No. Unless it's a useful activity Mum thinks it's a waste of time."

"Hmm, what about a pet? Having something to look after would suit her and if it was a puppy we could enrol her in training classes and she'd meet people on walks."

"No. It's a good idea in theory, but I can't see her with a dog. I wanted one when I was little and … oh!"

"What?"

"It was a case of over my dead body! Well not quite, but I had asthma and being near animals made it worse, plus we probably couldn't have afforded the food and vet bills."

"But you've grown out of the asthma and money's not such a problem now. Leave it with me."

A few weeks after Mum's cruise, Steve and Janine took her to a fundraising day at an animal shelter. They tried their luck on the tombola and guess the weight of the cake, enjoyed the refreshments and stroked the various animals in need of good homes. Steve, as tactfully as he could, mentioned the lack of any allergic reaction on his part.

It was hard to know if Mum was tempted to adopt an animal herself but she clearly wasn't unfeeling about their plight. When her name was read out as a raffle prize winner she requested the rowing machine she'd won be auctioned to raise further funds. The organisers thanked her profusely.

"Oh get away with you," Mum said. "Besides if I tried that contraption, the next time anyone saw it would probably be under my dead body."

When that didn't end the thanks, she edged away from the crowd listening to the results and went back to the animals in their pens. Or rather to one particular dog.

"Janine look, Mum likes that one."

"Yes, she was making quite a fuss of it earlier too."

"It's not a puppy so it's less likely to find a home. If we told her it'd be put down if no one adopted it, I reckon we could talk her into it."

Janine took a deep breath, crossed her arms and said, "If you want to manipulate her like that you'll have to do it across my dead body!"

"Janine!"

"I mean it, Steve. I know you're worried about her. So am I and I do think it would be good for her to have a dog, but it absolutely has to be her decision."

"I suppose you're right. It just seemed like the perfect solution."

"Maybe it is, but we won't push her. Let's tell her we're concerned about her being lonely and suggest she think about adopting the dog and she can make up her own mind."

"Who is she?" Mum asked. "That cat's mother?"

"No, Mum. Mine. We have a suggestion."

"Yes, I heard. Janine's right, pushing me into anything is a very bad idea."

Steve hung his head. "Yes, Mum I know. Sorry."

"I should think so. The same goes for doing things without thinking them through."

"How about we go and see if there's any tea and cake left and we can talk about it," Janine suggested.

"Good idea… but first I think I'll just go and see little Fudge again and maybe you could go and ask what the adoption procedure is, just as a matter of interest?"

24. Understandings And Misunderstandings

Ronald was startled by the phone ringing. A few months back it had been a common occurrence, but it rarely rang now, especially not in the daytime.

"Mr Sands?"

"Yes, that's right."

The caller introduced himself and the company he represented in that unintelligible way people develop when they're used to repeating the same phrase over and over. Ronald did catch something about an accident not being his fault.

"Of course it wasn't my fault," he said. He was old, not stupid.

"Exactly. And why should you suffer when someone else is to blame?"

"It was just an accident. No one is to blame. People go up and down those steps all the time without any problems."

The caller continued talking and it didn't take Ronald long to realise the younger man didn't actually know anything about the accident. Ronald guessed it might be a scam of some kind. Whether it was or not, they'd called the wrong person.

Ronald went into the kitchen to make a cup of tea and heard the couple who'd recently moved next door were having an argument. He didn't mean to listen, but the walls were paper thin and his kettle was slow to boil. The boy seemed to be complaining about the girl's job. Something about it not being right and having to do what people wanted.

"That's only a problem if... " then something Ronald missed as the kettle boiled. "Besides, I'd hate being inside all day. I have to get out."

Then it seemed she did go out, or perhaps it was the boy. In any case a door slammed. Ronald glanced at the clock and was surprised to see it was only quarter to nine. Breakfast seemed a long time ago and he'd already washed up after that. What was he going to do all day?

He thought about the telephone call and being asked why he should suffer. He'd twisted his ankle, slipping on the stairs up to his flat. It had been very painful at the time and uncomfortable for weeks afterwards, but he wasn't still suffering now. There was no reason he couldn't take a good long walk, he'd just got into the habit of catching a bus anywhere he needed to go, and staying in the rest of the time. Like his neighbour, he decided he had to get out for a while.

He'd start off by going into town. By following the bus route, he could easily change his mind and catch the number 57 if walking the whole way proved too tiring for him or made his ankle sore.

First though he had a shave, something he usually only bothered with on Monday when he went shopping. Afterwards it took him some time to decide what to wear. When he went to the supermarket it didn't matter much as he generally pulled his long, thin raincoat on over the top in case he got caught in a shower. It was a lovely clear day, so he shouldn't need that. Ronald ironed a pair of trousers and a shirt to go with the sweater his sister had knitted for him years ago.

The walk took a long time because Ronald stopped to sit on every bench he saw. It was good to feel the sun on his face and he had no need to rush back to his flat. Watching people hurry by, and looking at the different homes and gardens, was far more interesting. He caught snatches of conversation, much of it from students, but understood very little. Even those he was sure really were speaking English used so much modern slang it might as well have been a foreign language to Ronald.

By the time he reached town it was eleven o'clock and Ronald was more than ready for another cup of tea. Almost the moment he thought that, a sign advertising tea and a toasted teacakes for £2.50 attracted his attention. The Hot Kettle café was quite busy, but Ronald spotted an empty table and sat down. No one paid him any attention, despite him doing his best to look ready to order. It was difficult to see who was staff and who were customers as no one wore a uniform and everyone seemed busy.

Eventually a girl approached and gave him a lovely smile. "I love that sweater. Really retro!"

Ronald recognised that voice; it was his neighbour. Of course a waitress had to do as people asked, but it seemed a perfectly suitable job for a young lady. Why her young man was so against it Ronald couldn't understand, but he did know the meaning of 'retro'. That seemed to refer to things which were old, but in a good way.

"Thank you. I like to think it suits me."

"It's really cool."

Ronald knew what that meant too, but he smiled and

said, "Actually it's rather warm."

The girl giggled and asked him where he'd got it as she'd like to buy one for her boyfriend.

As he explained it had been made for him and she was suitably impressed by his sister's skill, Ronald gradually realised the waitress wasn't his neighbour, just someone who sounded similar.

"Would you mind if I took a couple of pictures, just in case I find someone who can knit?" she asked.

Ronald agreed and stood so she could take clear shots.

"Thanks a lot," she said and turned away.

"Excuse me, but might I have a cup of tea and toasted teacake?"

She glanced back at him, shrugged, then said, "Yeah, all right then."

Ronald was puzzled. Perhaps the special offer had been one of those just for early mornings and he'd ordered a bit too late, but it seemed the right sort of thing for elevenses and it was only just gone the hour.

It wasn't until Ronald attempted to pay for his snack and was told that everything was paid for when it left the counter, he realised his mistake. There were no waitresses and he'd asked a total stranger, a young girl, to buy him a drink and something to eat! She was no longer in the café and a walk up and down the High Street revealed no trace of her.

Ronald decided to return the following day at the same time, in the hope of seeing her again and paying for whatever she would like to eat and drink in return. That idea cheered him up immensely; despite his discomfort over the misunderstanding he'd enjoyed his little outing and would be pleased to repeat it as well as gaining the opportunity to put things right.

The girl wasn't in the café the next day, nor the next, nor when he tried again exactly a week after he'd seen her. Maybe he would never have the chance to explain and thank her, but he'd keep on with his visits to the café. The exercise was doing him good and he enjoyed the food, especially once he started going a little later and having his lunch there. Proper roast dinners he had and delicious stews; the sort of things it hadn't seemed worth his while cooking for one.

Three weeks after seeing the offer for teacakes, Ronald noticed another sign quoting the price of £2.50. That one was smaller and stuck in a bucket of flowers. He couldn't give them to the girl he'd mistaken for a waitress, but he did know of another young lady who deserved some; his neighbour. It was thinking he'd been talking to her which led to Ronald's mistake and that in turn had led to him regularly going into town and as a result being much happier than he had for some time. The couple had been arguing again and Ronald thought he'd heard her crying.

Ronald couldn't say he'd heard the arguments, not without embarrassment all round, so he'd need another reason… Ah, of course!

He waited until it seemed the girl was alone and tapped on the door. "This may seem strange," he said, "but there's a young lady I want to thank and as I can't, I'd like to give these to you instead." He explained about his mix up in the café, leaving out his belief he'd recognised the voice. "I'd feel a little less guilty if you'd accept these, so at least I've repaid someone."

"Thank you, they're lovely. Would you like a cup of

tea?"

"That's very kind."

They spoke about the weather, the proposed refurbishments to their flats and taste in biscuits, before lapsing into silence.

"Do you have a job?" Ronald asked for lack of anything better to say.

"Hmmm, bit of a sore point. I'm a gopher on a building site."

"I beg your pardon?"

"Well, technically I'm a labourer, but I'm no stronger than I look so mostly I run errands."

"Ah, yes, gopher. Go for that and go for this?"

"You've got it. I quite like it. Keeps me fit and I'd hate to be stuck in an office or shop all day."

Of course, he'd heard her saying that she needed to get out. He thought she'd just meant away from the same four walls, because he'd recognised that need in himself, but she'd meant it in a different way.

"A sore point, you said?"

"My boyfriend doesn't like it. He's popped in a couple of times and heard some of the banter. The blokes tend to tease me and call me darling, things like that. Jeff got it into his head… Actually I'm not sure what he thinks goes on, but he didn't seem to believe that I spend my time fetching nails and brewing tea. We rowed about it."

"I'm sorry to hear that."

Ronald was sorry to hear them having another argument that evening. The boyfriend wanted to know who'd bought her the flowers.

"You don't trust me and wouldn't believe me if I told you."

Ronald, feeling horribly guilty, moved into the living room and switched on the television. He didn't hear more arguments, or anything else, from his neighbours for several days. Then he answered a knock on his door and saw the pair of them standing hand in hand.

"We've just come to say we're having an engagement party at the end of the month and to see if you'd like to come," the girl said.

"Yeah and to say thanks," said Josh. "It was you giving Jazz those flowers that got us talking and sorting things out."

Ronald was delighted at the news and to see them both so happy. He wasn't quite sure how the flowers came into it, but he was pleased to think that he'd brought happiness rather than more discord, as he'd feared.

"Congratulations both of you and thank you so much for the invitation." He wouldn't attend the party of course, noisy crowds and modern music didn't appeal, but it was nice that they'd asked.

He was thoughtful after his visitors had left. There had been a number of misunderstandings over the last few weeks. And some from further back. After the accident he'd been upset and defensive. He'd misunderstood some of the comments from his family and friends.

A few months ago, Ronald's son had said he shouldn't be on his own all the time. Now Ronald realised he hadn't meant he was incapable of looking after himself, just that he didn't want his father to feel lonely. Friends who'd said, 'Don't be a stranger' weren't complaining that for a time he'd been unable to travel to see them, but had been inviting him to keep in touch.

Ronald picked up the phone, then hesitated. Who should he ring first? One of his old cronies? There was a bus stop right outside the café and a train station round the corner. He'd suggest they meet there for tea and a toasted tea cake. First though he'd call his son to accept the offer to spend a week with him and his wife. If he picked the right time, his young neighbours would perfectly understand his absence from their party.

25. I Spy

"I spy with my little eye, something beginning with W," said ten-year-old Leo.

"Windscreen," Rowan guessed without stopping to think. It was right there in front of her, but she was supposed to let the kids win, wasn't she? To win them round. That's what a friend had advised, but Rowan wasn't so sure it was the right thing to do. You don't trick your way through a relationship, not if you want it to be one of mutual respect, love and trust.

"Yes," Leo sounded pleased.

"No." His older brother Max didn't.

"Ow!" from Leo, followed by, "No."

"No cheating," Howard, their dad, said. "It's Rowan's go now."

She'd rather he hadn't intervened. That could seem as though he were siding with her, rather than his boys. Still it did confirm she'd been right not to deliberately give unlikely answers to let them win. That was cheating, just as much as not allowing a correct answer to prevent her from being the victor. Although I Spy didn't really work like that, did it? It wasn't cumulative with just one winner.

Rowan spotted an ice cream van, parked up ahead. The traffic was moving so slowly that Howard, if he picked up on the clue, could pull in and let her out to buy some and it'd make very little difference to the overall journey time.

But was buying them treats a good idea? She didn't want to be seen to be trying to buy their affection… She was definitely overthinking this. People bought ice cream all the time, usually just because they liked it.

"I spy with my little eye, something beginning with I," she said.

"Ice cream!" both boys called immediately and very enthusiastically.

That was quicker even than her answer had been. Did they share a psychic bond?

"Let's have one, shall we?" she suggested.

"Yay! Ice cream so freezy, makes me sneezy," the boys chorused as Howard drove straight past the ice cream van.

"Dad, stop a minute!" That was Max.

"You missed the ice cream van," Leo explained.

Howard pulled over at the next opportunity.

"Ninety-nines all round?" Rowan offered.

"Yes please! They're the bestest."

"Thanks, Rowan."

"I'd rather have a can of something cold," Howard said.

No mind-reading going on there then. A lot of the time Rowan thought she knew how his kids felt, but that was less often the case with Howard. He liked her, that much was obvious. Sometimes she was certain it was more than that, that he felt about her as she did about him. What she needed was some kind of clear sign.

Howard took a long swallow of his drink, put the can in the cup holder, and restarted the car. He hadn't gone off ice cream then, but simply wanted to get them all to the beach as soon as possible. Those tiny little sacrifices he made for the boys, and her, were just one of the things she loved about him. He'd missed the second half of a semi-final football match to rescue her the time she ran out of petrol. When she'd realised Rowan had apologised.

"You've done me a big favour," he'd said. "Their performance was painful to watch." Maybe, but she'd only remembered about the match because his car radio was tuned in to the commentary.

As the others ate their ice creams, Max resumed the I Spy game. The next two words both started with L. There was sniggering from the boys, making Rowan guess they were trying to spell out rude words, just as they often did when playing Scrabble. She didn't discourage that. Having fun with words and getting creative seemed a far better way of encouraging an interest in English than telling them off.

She was proved right. 'Yellow,' was the next word and the boys seemed very pleased with themselves. Rowan pretended she hadn't noticed what the first five letters had spelled out.

"Who's go is it now?" she asked.

"Mine. I spy, little eye, starts with O."

Max quickly guessed 'orange.'

"Ugly!" Max declared, when everyone failed to guess U. "Ugly like Leo. Ha ha ha."

The reaction to that brotherly taunt, and subsequent 'Ow' were very half-hearted. Today it seemed something more important than their usual squabbles was holding their attention.

"Spy, little eye, M," Max said.

They were both oddly determined to persevere with the

I Spy game. Rowan had been right; there was something weird about it. They were a little old for it really and she'd discovered that them simultaneously wanting to do something educational or helpful usually meant a hidden agenda. Offering to clear the tea table whenever they all visited her on a Sunday meant they'd 'dispose' of any cake that she'd thought would be left for her coffee break the next day. Asking her if they could all watch a 'really interesting' documentary on TV usually had something to do with the fact it finished after the time Howard usually sent them up to bed.

That, she was sure, was just a childhood wish to stay up late, not an attempt to prevent her being alone with their dad. Actually sometimes they did things which meant the pair of them spent more time together, such as suggesting Rowan stay over last night, so in the morning they could drive straight to the beach, instead of calling round to pick her up on the way. She'd had a feeling that something was up for a few days. Now, what could it be? Oh yes, Rowan over thinking things. Again.

Maybe they were teasing her? She didn't mind that – it proved they liked her and were relaxed enough around her to treat her as they did each other and their dad. She'd like a permanent role in the lives of all three. Sometimes it felt that would happen. She'd been seeing Howard for over a year. He was often keen to spend time with her alone and to include her in family activities, talk about the future as though she'd be there for it. Then, just as she started to feel she was no longer on the edge of things, he'd back off. It was unsettling for her and surely for the boys too.

She'd not been paying attention to the I Spy game and a "Daaaad" informed her Howard wasn't playing it to their liking either. Rowan made an effort to concentrate. There were two Rs one after the other and then another Y, which took ages to guess as nobody could think of anything. The choice of letters must mean something. The way the boys were laughing confirmed that, as did the piece of paper she realised they'd been referring to.

"I spy with my little eye, something beginning with D," said Max.

"Dunce!" replied Leo. "You saw yourself in the mirror! Ha ha ha. Ow! Ow! Ow!"

Rowan glanced back and saw Max had rolled up the piece of paper and was whacking his brother with it. Leo, as usual was over reacting to what was only a very token effort at revenge for the latest insult. Such behaviour was typical of them and seemed to bring them closer together rather than making them fall out. Under normal circumstances, Rowan would have ignored it, but she was sure these weren't normal circumstances and that piece of paper could give her a clue about what was going on. Seizing her chance, she snatched it from Max's grasp.

Oddly Max didn't try to get it back, or say "That's mine." Leo didn't cheer that his brother's weapon had been taken from him. Both boys sat back quietly, waiting.

Rowan uncurled the sheet of paper, turned it the right way up and read the simple message. She closed her eyes for a moment and read it again. It still said, 'Will You Marry Dad'.

She glanced at Howard. His concentration was on the road. She couldn't tell if he was aware of what his boys had been up to. A quick look at them showed they were still waiting for her to react.

"Are you serious?" she asked.

"Yes." They said it together, quietly and with sincerity.

Rowan reached back and just about managed to grasp Leo's left and Max's right hands. "That's really sweet of you both and I'd really like to say yes, but it's your dad who has to make the decision… and do the asking."

"He wants to ask you, but he said if you said no then we'd lose you. We don't want that to happen," Max explained.

"So we thought we'd ask you instead," Leo added.

"Good idea," she said.

"Ask who what?" Howard asked.

"Ask Rowan if she'll marry you. We've been doing it with the I Spy letters."

"Oh!" Howard said. "And what did Rowan say?"

"That it's a good idea, but you have to ask."

He glanced at her. "Did you?"

"Something like that."

"Will you, Rowan? Will you please marry me?"

"I spy with my little eye …" Rowan looked around her, hoping to spot a yak, yacht or even a yeti.

Thank you for reading this book. I hope you enjoyed it. If you did, I'd really appreciate it if you could spare the time to leave a short review on Amazon and/or Goodreads.

To learn more about my writing life, hear about new releases and get a free short story, sign up to my newsletter – subscribepage.io/ItLSNa or you can find the link on my website patsycollins.co.uk

<u>More books by Patsy Collins</u>

Novels

Firestarter
Escape To The Country
A Year And A Day
Paint Me A Picture
Leave Nothing But Footprints
Acting Like A Killer

Little Mallow cosy mystery series

Disguised Murder and Community Spirit
in Little Mallow
Dependable Friends and Deceitful Neighbours
in Little Mallow
Deadly Words and Innocent Gossip in Little Mallow

Non-fiction

From Story Idea To Reader
(co-written with Rosemary J. Kind)

A Year Of Ideas:
365 sets of writing prompts and exercises

Short story collections

Criminal Intent
Crime In Mind

Over The Garden Fence
Up The Garden Path
Through The Garden Gate
In The Garden Air
Beyond The Garden Wall

No Family Secrets
Can't Choose Your Family
Keep It In The Family
Family Feeling
Happy Families

All That Love Stuff
With Love And Kisses
Lots Of Love
Love Is The Answer

Just A Job
Perfect Timing
Dressed To Impress
Coffee & Cake
Not A Drop To Drink
Making A Move
A Clean Bill Of Health

Slightly Spooky Stories I
Slightly Spooky Stories II
Slightly Spooky Stories III
Slightly Spooky Stories IV
Slightly Spooky Stories V

9 781914 339295